ABOUT THE AUTHOR

Well where do I begin?

To start off with, I'm a 54 year old gay guy living in England, UK and I live with my soul mate, a very special man indeed.

In the past I have only ever read other guys works but one day I decided that for once I would like to direct the plot. So what appeared to be a quick bash out on the keyboard for a couple of pages story proved to be the beginnings of an interesting new hobby.

I hope that you will enjoy reading my stories as much as I do writing them!

Other titles available:

A Biker's Tale – Part 1 (The Initiation of Danny Challetts)
A Biker's Tale – Part 2 (Running with the Pack)
A Chance Encounter
Army Bad Lads
Austin Mannuelo: The Confession of a Male Escort
Becoming a Model Patient
Diary of a Prison Officer – Part 1
Diary of a Prison Officer – Part 2
Diary of a Prison Officer – Part 3
Doing Time
Erotic Short Stories
Lost Innocence
Second Time Around
Shooting Stars
Summer Camp
The Calling
The Kidnapping of Ryan Millshank
The Naked Waiter

ISBN: 9798363618529
Imprint: Independently published

All characters contained within are entirely fictional; any similarity to any real or fictional person living or deceased is totally unintentional. Do not read this story if you do not enjoy reading about consensual sexual activities of an exhibitionist nature. Otherwise read on......

CHAPTER LISTINGS

A BIKER'S TALE – PART 1 (THE INITIATION OF DANNY CHALLETS)

Chapter 1 – Wishing can be dangerous
Chapter 2 – A date with destiny
Chapter 3 – The morning after the night before
Chapter 4 – An invitation that's hard to refuse
Chapter 5 – An introduction to the clan
Chapter 6 – The tattoo parlour
Chapter 7 – The training begins
Chapter 8 – Stretching to new limits
Chapter 9 – Initiation time
Chapter 10 – Celebrations for a new beginning

A BIKER'S TALE – PART 2 (RUNNING WITH THE PACK)

Chapter 1 – The return to Colonie
Chapter 2 – Getting down to business
Chapter 3 – Tattoo time
Chapter 4 – Late night entertainment
Chapter 5 – Camera, roll, action!
Chapter 6 – Reunion at Gettysburg
Chapter 7 – A cry for help
Chapter 8 – The trap is sprung
Chapter 9 – Dog training begins
Chapter 10 – Attitude correction
Chapter 11 – Breaking in the dogs
Chapter 12 – The tail that wags the dog
Chapter 13 – Of dogs and bears, the training continues
Chapter 14 – Three in a bed
Chapter 15 – On tour
Chapter 16 – The long arm of the law

Chapter 1 – Wishing can be dangerous

Have you ever heard of the saying "be careful what you wish, for it may come true"?

Well for me the saying proved all too true, as my following tale will demonstrate beyond a doubt. Don't get me wrong I wouldn't change my life now for anything but on one fateful day this summer my life went from being safe and predictable (some might say boring) to exciting and at times scary.

But I'm jumping ahead of myself, let me start at the beginning and introduce myself to you. My name is Danny Challetts, aged twenty four, medium height and slim with close cropped auburn hair. My best feature I would say are my eyes for they are a tawny colour and in bright sunlight look golden. My worst feature has to be my skin for it is white at the best of times except for when it is a painful red when I have been out in the sun too long. As a kid at school I my class mates called me a vampire because my skin was so pale and I didn't like the hot summer sun. However when I complained about the teasing my mother just used to scold me and say that I should be proud of my Irish ancestry and stand up to the bullies.

Once I left school the teasing stopped and the colour of my skin was no longer an issue when it came to getting men into my bed. Oh yes, by the way I am gay and proud of it. I have my own apartment in Glens Falls, New York State, which I rent cheaply because it's on top of the grocery shop where I work as the assistant manager. The job title sounds grand doesn't it? But in reality there's only the manager, myself and a young girl who works weekends.

My life at the moment is not quite in a rut but it is definitely following a regular routine. I work five days per week on a changing shift pattern, when not at work I'm generally hanging out with my two best mates Perry Seaham and Lewis Devling. We've known each other since school and came out of the closet within weeks of each other. I like to think of myself as being the butchest of the three but I'm sure if you asked them they would argue otherwise! For ages I have been moaning that there's no fresh talent on the local scene and I'm getting so desperate that I might have to go cruising the straight joints! At night I would lay in bed idling wishing for something, anything to happen which might spice things up a little for me, after all I'm in my twenties and not getting any younger.

The powers that be must have been listening to my prayers for one Saturday morning as I was doing some household chores my mobile phone rang. Glad for a break I flipped the screen up to find that Perry was calling, strange I thought for at weekends he's not usually out of bed before mid-day.

"Hi ya. What's up?" I asked as I continued dusting the window sills in the lounge.

"Are you busy?" Perry asked outright.

"Not really. Only doing chores" I replied.

"How do you fancy going to the Honaw Motorcycle Rally up at Lake George today?"

"Oh, I dunno. You know I don't like being around all those Hells Angel type guys, they scare me a little!" I replied sounding a bit girly even to my own ears.

"Look" he continued, not put off in the slightest "what else are you going to do? Think of all those macho men showing off on their motorbikes, all that grease and testosterone."

"Well, as you put it like that, I could be persuaded but only on the condition that Lewis comes along to protect me" I replied knowing full well that Lewis would not want to be left out.

"Yes! You're the greatest mate in the whole wide world!" Perry cried down the phone, clearly pleased with my decision.

"I know and I'm the only one with a car. What time do you want me to pick you guys up?" I replied a little smugly.

"How about half an hour from now at my house, Lewis is just getting changed.........." he trailed off.

"You little beggars! I'll see you two in half an hour then" I said as I burst out laughing realising that I had been manipulated into this by Perry.

Hanging up on Perry I quickly put the cleaning stuff away and dashed into the bedroom to choose my outfit for the rally. Well, you never who you might bump into at a rally, it could even be the man of your dreams. Hmmph, fat chance! I thought as I rummaged through my wardrobe searching for clothes suitable for hot weather but also offering protection from the sun. In the end I chose a cream linen shirt and bleached jeans with matching trainers, finished with a white baseball cap to keep the sun out of my eyes. Inspecting myself from all angles in my full length mirror, I was satisfied with the casual effect of the ensemble and that I still looked young and attractive (modesty is not a trait I possess).

Fifteen minutes I pulled up outside Perry's house, actually his parents for he's not left home yet, and tooted my horn to announce my arrival. I nearly died with embarrassment when I saw Perry and Lewis appear from the front door. Perry was wearing a black muscle vest, black boots, pinky purple camouflage combats and matching baseball cap. Lewis was dressed similarly in a turquoise muscle vest, black boots and pale blue camouflage combats. His head was uncovered because he's so proud of his blonde hair and hates to flatten it with hats. My expression must have been comical for they both laughed and waved exaggeratedly which only increased the embarrassment factor still further! I just shook my head in resignation, there simply was no point complaining as it would only make them worse.

Concentrating on driving enabled me to forget about their outfits and the conversation quickly turned to discussing the types of guys we might see at the rally along with the things Perry wanted to do. Driving northbound on Interstate 87 towards Lake George I noticed that traffic was heavier than normal going our way and I wondered if they were heading for the same destination as us. From the rear of the car Perry was bouncing around in excitement every time a motorbike overtook us, for all his campness he just loved those two wheeled machines and of course their male riders. It seemed the whole world was converging on Lake George that day and it took us nearly half an hour of queuing to find a parking spot near to the rally site and then had to queue to pay the entrance fee. But it was worth the wait, the site was much bigger than I was expecting with a large trade stand area and huge main arena. Dotted all over the place were food and drink facilities as well as non-biker themed amusement areas for families with children. The place was already crowded with people and it seemed to me that the every section of society was represented not just the hardened bikers.

As we meandered amongst the trade stands I relaxed and even enjoyed myself as Lewis and Perry inspected the different makes and models of motorbikes on display. I chuckled to myself seeing the look of condescension on the seller's faces slip as they realised that the two obviously gay guys knew their bikes and became almost buddies as they discussed the mechanical and technical aspects of the bikes in question. I had to walk away though when they started flirting with the sellers, I didn't want to be present when the macho guys realised that they were being hit on nor give the game away by laughing out loud. Each time they'd catch me up grinning like idiots and more often than not they'd be holding business cards as trophies. A couple of hours passed very quickly and before I knew it my stomach was rumbling from hunger, I was not the only one for as mine rumbled again Perry announced that he fancied a hot dog as he was starving and headed straight for the nearest hot dog stand.

Lewis and I ran to catch up with him, standing there in the queue we started looking around to see if we could spot any eye candy. Perry is a natural man hunter and within seconds was poking us both in the ribs and pointing with his head in the direction of a nearby stall where a guy stood with his back to us talking to a female stall holder. The guy is question seemed to sense our attention and looked over in our direction. Perry nearly came in his pants there and then! I must admit he was a very handsome man if a little older than the guys I normally hooked up with. I'd put him in his late thirties to early forties, a great bear of a man standing at over six and a half feet tall wearing black leather trousers and matching waistcoat over a tight white muscle vest. From his posture and demeanour he was clearly used to being in charge. His head was shaved except for an inch long strip of black hair running from his forehead to the nape of his neck gelled in a Mohican style. Facially he was clean shaven except for a pointed goatee beard grown to about two inches long again it was black. His large dark brown eyes had a dangerous glint to them and a shiver ran down my spine as his eyes met mine. He held my gaze for what seemed an eternity before with a slight smile he turned away to resume his conversation with the stall holder.

Perry was visibly deflated; for once he had failed to gain a guy's attention even though he had been trying his best to do so. He was too wrapped up in his own misery to realise that it was me who had received the eye contact and being the friend I am I decided not to tell him of this fact. As we made our way to the main arena with hot dogs and drinks in hand we gently teased Perry about him losing his touch. Watching the motor racing in the arena Lewis announced that he didn't know what the fuss was all about, the bloke looked like a whole lot of trouble and best off avoided. Neither Perry nor myself made a comment.

Later that afternoon, having grown bored of watching the displays and just a little irritated by the crowds, we wandered down to the shoreline dock where a river steamer was docked and taking on passengers. Curious to find out what was going on we picked up our pace and joined the back of the queue while we read the notice board.

After a quick discussion we decided to buy tickets for the two hour boat cruise on the lake, it was something none of us had done before and sounded like fun. As I reached into my pocket to retrieve my cash I felt someone standing close behind me. Turning round, with my hand still in my pocket, I was met by the sight of a muscular hairy chest inches from my face. Tilting my head back I looked up at the heavily tanned face looking down at me and straight into the eyes of the guy I had seen while queuing up for my hot dog. With anyone else I would have come out with a flippant remark about standing so close to me. But there was something mesmerising about him and I just stood there rooted to the spot taking in the face before me and the feint smell of sandalwood. Reflexively I smiled up at him and my heart skipped a beat when he smiled back, my smile faltered a little however when I felt him put his arm around my waist and pull me closer to him. Then before I could react I felt the fingers of his other hand push their way inside the waistband of my jeans before pulling back just as quickly. Still smiling the guy released his hold on my waist and sauntered off back in the direction of the rally grounds without once looking back.

Still stunned and unable to believe what had just occurred I failed to notice that the queue had moved on until Perry called out to me. Shaking my head to get my brain working again I ran to catch up with my two friends as they were about to board the steamer. The boat was already packed by the time we climbed on but fortune was smiling on us as we managed to find three seats not taken at the front of the boat. As I sat down I felt something dig into my thigh, looking around to make sure that no one was watching I discretely slipped my hand down my trousers and found what had been digging into my leg. I was surprised to find a business card in my hand, so that must have been what that guy had been doing. I always knew that I should have been a detective!

With Lewis and Perry preoccupied watching the passing seafront scenery and mountain backdrop I was able to examine business card. On the front it read "Kurt Honaw, Events Coordinator" above a motorcycle in profile and American Indian style motifs all around the border. Turning the card over there was a simple hand-written message on the reverse "Call me" along with his mobile number. Raising my eyebrows I smiled to myself before tucking the card into my back pocket for safekeeping. I then turned my attention to enjoying the boat trip and spending the time joking and messing around with my two best mates, for some reason the day seemed to have got a whole lot better.

Chapter 2 – A date with destiny

That evening, having dropped Perry and Lewis back off at their homes, I drove home with my head in turmoil about the card in my pocket. What should I do with it? The sensible half of me was saying to tear the card up and throw it away for he might be trouble as Lewis had stated. Whereas the adventurous half was saying give him a call, let your hair down and see what happens. I swung between those two points of views like a pendulum. It wasn't until I recalled how much I'd been wishing for something exciting to happen that I finally made my mind up. I decided to seize the opportunity and invite some adventure into my life.

Feeling nervous but also a little excited I dialled the number on the back of the card but it just rang and rang. I was about to give up, thinking it was an omen, when I heard a gruff 'hello'. Again a shiver ran down my spine at the sound of his voice. What was it about this man? I wondered to myself before with a slight shakiness to my voice I said hello back and told him who I was. That was the beginning of an hour long call during which I seemed to reveal so much about myself, my dreams and aspirations but now I think about it I can't remember Kurt disclosing much about himself at all. Even so, I felt I was a good judge of character and he seemed genuine enough for me to agree to meet up with him later. He told me that he would pick me up on his motorbike in an hour's time and that we'd be going out for a couple of drinks and see how we get on.

With that agreed I quickly showered to wash the day's sweat off and shaved to make myself smart again. Then came the ordeal of knowing quite what it wear, I wanted something manly to match the character of the guy I was going for a drink with. Well I didn't possess anything made of leather (other than my shoes and Doc Martin boots) so black denim jeans would have to do with a rather cliché tartan lumberjack shirt and my black DM boots. Standing before the full length mirror, just like I had this morning, I carefully inspected my appearance to make sure everything was in order. Satisfied I walked through to the lounge and looked out of the window onto the main road waiting for Kurt to arrive.

I heard him coming before I could see him for the roar of his bike was a giveaway, he rode slowly obviously looking for the door numbers until he spotted mine. I was impressed for I had been expecting him to look like a hell's angel, but no, he was dressed from head to toe in expensive professional black leathers and matching helmet with darkened face guard. Coming to a halt he sat astride his bike, took off his helmet before taking his mobile out of his pocket and dialled, obviously my number as my phone started ringing.

Smiling I picked my phone up and answered "Hi ya!"

"Come on down. I want to take you for a ride" was all Kurt said before hanging up.

There was something in the way he emphasised the word 'take' which caught my attention and made my loins stir. I didn't need a second telling for I was already out of my front door and racing down the communal stairs which led onto the main street. By the time I got to the bike Kurt had removed a spare helmet from one of the panniers and was held it out to me while giving me a very obvious once over. He must have liked what he saw because he nodded with a smile and turned the bike's engine on as I pulled the helmet on over my head. I just had time to climb on behind him and put my arms around his waist before he revved the engine and we were off!

I don't know what was more thrilling, holding him close to me in a very intimate way or watching the scenery flash by as we sped up the interstate back to Lake George. Either way I enjoyed the ride and was just a little disappointed when we pulled up in front of a lake front bar. Dismounting we made our way over to the bar and removed our helmets just in time for the bar man to greet Kurt by name before he nodded to me with a smile. Kurt ordered a beer for me and a soda water for himself before leading us to a nearby bench. Sitting side by side we people watched while we sipped our drinks and talked. Once again I found myself divulging more personal stuff while Kurt only told me scant information about himself. He was so charming and persuasive that at the time I didn't notice the imbalance in the information flow. After I'd had a couple of beers I was definitely getting tipsy and any barriers that I might have had up were definitely down. So when Kurt invited me to back to his place for a coffee I was more than happy to accept.

Downing the last of our drinks we bid goodnight to the bar man and climbed back on to Kurt's bike for the short couple of miles ride to the camp site where he was staying. We pulled up in front of a surprisingly large trailer, I had been expecting it to be of the static variety but Kurt assured me that it was fully mobile and after the rally here in Lake George it would be towed to the next rally venue. Stowing both our helmets into the panniers Kurt led me up the steps and unlocking the front door, into the main living/dining area of the trailer. I was impressed not only by the size and contents of the room but also by the fact that it was clean and tidy. It was clearly a man's place, with no feminine touches anywhere, the two brown leather sofas were slightly worn but very sturdy which were separated by an equally sturdy wooden coffee table. Facing the sofas on a solid wall was a large flat screen TV surrounded by framed photos of motorbikes and their riders, both static and in action. Each of the windows had vertical blinds which Kurt closed to allow us privacy from our neighbours. Then he gave me a whistle stop tour of the rest of the trailer, there were four doors off a small internal hall, to the left was the shower room and next to that the toilet. Immediately in front was Kurt's bedroom which ran the width of the trailer, it was the bigger of the two bedrooms. Inside it contained a double bed with overhead storage units and bedside cabinets along with a wardrobe and full length mirror hung on the back of the door. Snug but manageable Kurt assured me. The fourth door, which remained firmly shut, led into the second bedroom and was occupied by Logan Babet, an employee of the company and personal friend of Kurt's.

Tour over we returned to the lounge and I relaxed on a sofa watching Kurt as he expertly prepared two large and strong espresso coffees for us. Sitting opposite me as we sipped our coffees Kurt pointed to each of the photos and told me a little bit of history to each one, before quite casually slipping in a question which nearly made me spray coffee all over him!

"So Danny" Kurt asked taking another sip from his cup "have you ever gone skinny dipping by moonlight?"

Catching me totally off guard I spluttered into my coffee cup and blushed bright red before shaking my head in place of an answer.

"In that case you don't know what you've been missing! It's a lovely warm evening, the lake will be beautiful and as it's late no one will be around. How do you fancy it?" he asked but was already rising from his seat.

"Sure, why not? I'll try anything once" I replied trying to sound more confident than I actually felt.

Locking the door behind us we walked through the camp site downhill to the shore of the lake. As Kurt had correctly assumed there was nobody around at this time of night, presumably they were asleep in bed as very few trailers had any lights on. Having found a suitable spot on the shore and without looking around Kurt casually removed his clothes. First to come off was his tight T-shirt allowing me to see his tanned, hairy muscular torso and as he turned slightly I saw for the first time the tattoos that covered his back and the tops of his biceps. Unfortunately in the dim light I was unable to make out the intricate designs. Then with practised ease he removed his biker's boots and stuffed his socks into them, next his leather trousers were smoothly undone and pushed down to his ankles before he stepped out of them. Without a trace of hesitation he slipped his fingers into the waistband of his boxer shorts and pulled them down. This was the first time that I had ever seen such a masculine guy totally naked before me. His legs were just as tanned as his face and torso but the tan line stopped just beneath his buttocks and started again above his waist, his cheeks and crotch looked white in comparison. Unconsciously with one hand he adjusted his cock and balls allowing them to swing freely before he turned and waded into the inky black water until he was in up to his waist. I was frozen to the spot unable to take my eyes off his beautiful body which moved with all the strength and confidence of a mountain lion.

My reverie was broken when Kurt turned round and expressed surprise that I was still standing there fully clothed. I felt more than a little embarrassed at having been caught out staring at him so I grinned and started to strip. Being naturally shy about my body I could not help but look around to make sure no one was watching before removing my pants, the last article of clothing to come off. In the bright moonlight my naked body glowed an almost luminous white which only made me feel more self-conscious as I felt I was like a shining beacon in the darkness. At least it spurred me on to join Kurt in the cold water of the lake, who, having watched me undress with just as much interest as I had watched him was now swimming out into the lake. I have to admit that there was something sensual about feeling the water flow all around my intimate parts as I swam to catch up with Kurt.

Finally he stopped and I caught up with him, treading water we turned slowly taking in the view of the wooded shorelines, the starry sky above us and the distant town of Lake George off to the left, still well lit at this time of night. Like two teenage boys we floated around for a while just savouring the experience and pretending that we were the only people in the world. Then treading water again Kurt took me in one arm and started to kiss me amorously, his beard prickled me initially but I quickly got accustomed to it. Mainly because I got distracted by his tongue which forcefully invaded my mouth, rising to the challenge I kissed him back just as passionately. But try as I might I was just not strong enough to get my tongue into his mouth. Breaking away momentarily he chuckled darkly before he ravaged my mouth with his tongue once more. At the same time I felt a hand slide down between us and started to caress my balls before it stroked my cock to full erection.

I was getting close to the point of no return, when perhaps sensing this Kurt broke away from me and swam off in the direction of the shore. Frustrated beyond belief I swam after him trying to think of a way to ask why had he stopped and left me ready to burst. Naturally he got to shore first and by the time I swam ashore he was already lying face up with his hands beneath his head on the grassy shoreline allowing the night breeze dry him off. His cock was rock hard and the sight of this drove all rational thoughts out of my head. He gestured for me to join him on the ground, which I did although I was shivering slightly from the cold. Then not caring who may have been around Kurt gave me a lingering kiss before slowly and teasingly he kissed me all the way down my body until he reached my throbbing erection. His blow job was out of this world, not once did his teeth scrape me and he seemed to intuitively know all of my sensitive spots. My body was jerking and my head rolling from side to side in ecstasy by the time I lost control sending jet after jet of pent up jism shooting down his willing throat. He continued sucking until I could shoot no more and my cock had shrunk back to normal size. With a contented grin he kissed me on my lips (which left me with trace of my own taste in my mouth) before rising to his feet and gathered up his clothes.

Following his lead I gathered up my clothes expecting to get dressed again but Kurt apparently had other plans as he told me not to worry as no one's around and that I'd only have to take them off again. Now I liked the sound of that! So off we walked as casual as you like, still starkers carrying our clothes rolled up in a bundle beneath our arms, in the direction of our trailer. We talked in hushed tones about the trailers we were passing and who the occupied them when from round a corner two extremely drunk teenage girls appeared without warning. They immediately giggled and whistled at the sight of our naked bodies before making it clear what they would like to do with us, yuk!

Kurt simply shook his head, said "not tonight girls" and carried on walking making no attempt to cover himself up. I was really embarrassed, I covered my tackle with my clothes and smiled sheepishly, I walked a little faster to put distance between me and the girls. I could hear their laughter all the way back to Kurt's trailer and was only too glad to run up the couple of steps to the front door and disappear within.

However my relief was short lived for as I closed the door behind me and looked round I realised that we weren't alone in the trailer. Sitting on each sofa were two guys who had been watching the baseball game on the TV but on our entrance they both looked in our direction, one with raised eyebrows, the other with a welcoming smile to me and a nod to Kurt. I could feel myself blushing all over again at yet another embarrassing situation, well for me at least for Kurt didn't seem phased in the slightest. Putting an arm around my shoulder he pulled me to his side before he introduced me to Logan whose smile grew even bigger as he stood up and shook my hand before asking me if I'd like a beer in a strong French Canadian accent. As I nodded my head in acceptance of the offer Kurt announced that he'd like one too and high fived Logan as he walked past. Kurt then introduced me to the other guy who was still sitting on the sofa with a slightly amused look on his face.

"Danny, I'd like you to meet my friend Wayne, we've known each for many years" Kurt said matching Wayne's smile.

I shook Wayne's offered hand and said "Pleased to meet you, sorry about our state of undress, I hope we haven't offended you."

Chuckling Wayne replied "Not in the slightest, Kurt always did have good taste. To be honest nothing Kurt does surprises me any longer."

"Hey! Less of that sort of talk please" Kurt said with a hurt expression on his face "my young cub here will get the wrong impression of me."

 "Cub?" Wayne and I said in unison.

As we glanced at each other in surprise Kurt shrugged his shoulders and replied "that's what I said" before he took the two bottles of beer Logan held out towards him. Then as if to draw a line under the subject he steered me into the hall and then to his room before calling over his shoulder "See you later guys!"

As the door shut behind me I asked "so what does cub mean?"

"It's a term of endearment that's all" Kurt murmured reassuringly as he dropped his clothing on the floor in a pile, then took mine and did the same.

I stood there for a minute just taking in the sight of his gorgeous body, it was everything mine wasn't. He was muscular where I was slim (okay skinny), he was hairy where I had little, he was tanned where I was white, he was well hung while I was average in comparison. The appraisal mentally made me doubt why such a handsome man would hit on someone ordinary like me, but my body was not concerned about such matters. Within a few seconds I was standing to attention and my feet moved of their own accord until I was standing in front of him looking up at his smiling face.

In a move which caught me by surprise Kurt abruptly bent down, slung me over his shoulder in a fireman's lift and carried me over to his bed. Laying me down on my back, he quickly crawled on top pinning me down with the weight of his body. Slowly he wriggled himself along until our erect cocks lay side by side, then lowering his head he kissed me all over my face, neck and shoulders with the occasional nibble. At the same time he gently thrust his pelvis into mine making our cocks to rub against one another. I made little whimpering noises in response to the pleasurable sensations he was causing and I found my legs wrapping themselves around his waist to pull him even closer to me.

Then he turned his attention to my mouth and with his tongue made love to it, sometimes gently sometimes roughly. I thought I was going to explode there and then! Perhaps sensing this Kurt pulled away from me, leant across the bed to his bedside cabinet and opened a drawer. Fumbling around he finally found what he was seeking and almost triumphantly held up a large tube of KY.

"I'm going to fuck you now" he said in an authoritive voice as he extricated himself from my legs.

Any thoughts of arguing his announcement simply didn't enter into my head.

"How do you want me?" slipped huskily from my lips.

"Roll over on to your front. I want to see those gorgeous white cheeks and that tight little hole of yours before I stretch it wide open."

Eagerly I complied with his instructions, laying face down I spread my legs wide and at the same time reached behind me pulling my cheeks apart. I felt cool air waft along my now exposed crack and anus.

"Okay?" I asked as I looked at Kurt from over my shoulder.

"Perfect, just perfect" he murmured as he knelt down between my outstretched legs.

I felt with a jolt the cold KY land on my hole, which puckered and quivered in response, as he gave the tube a big squeeze. With one finger he smeared it around my crack before pushing some of it inside my anus. I'm far from a virgin so I was able to easily accommodate his finger and wiggled my bum to indicate my enjoyment of the intrusion.

"Oh you want more eh?" Kurt asked with an amused tone to his voice.

"Yeah" I replied with my eyes closed.

With that a second finger joined the first and for several minutes those fingers slowly fucked me, alternating between corkscrewing and simple in and out motions. This continued until it was clear that I was totally relaxed, they then withdrew and the bed moved under Kurt's weight as he adjusted his position. Looking over at him I watched him as he liberally applied the KY to his hefty looking cock. From this angle it looked even bigger than when I was standing in front of him.

My expression must have revealed my thoughts because with a wink Kurt said

"Yes, you're right. I'm a big boy but I know that you can take this right up to the hilt. All you have to do is take deep breaths and relax."

Easier said than done I thought as his large cockhead pressed against my anal ring with a gentle but constant pressure. Slowly but surely, as I took deep breaths, I felt it stretch my ring ever wider for it had to be bigger than any dildo I had at home. Then with a tangible plop his head slipped past my ring which promptly clamped around his shaft.

"Easy tiger, relax that ring and let me in" Kurt whispered into my ear before playfully biting my shoulder.

As a distraction it worked, for while I yelped at his bites my ring relaxed its grip, allowing his cock to slide fully up inside my rectum until his balls were resting on mine.

"Aaargh!" I cried out in reaction to being impaled on his cock.

"Shush" Kurt murmured from behind me "the discomfort will go in a minute, just relax and trust me, I know what I'm doing."

I didn't have much option considering that I was pinned to the bed by his body and that my ring and rectum were being fully stretched by his huge cock, so I just grunted and buried my face in duvet beneath me. He remained motionless for a couple of minutes to allow me to get accustomed to the intrusion before slowly sliding his cock in and out of my backside. He never fully withdrew, leaving just his cockhead inside me before driving his cock back up my rectum until he could go no further. Slowly, almost imperceptibly the pace of the fucking increased until he was banging away like there was no tomorrow. Each thrust pushed me forward so I had to brace myself with my hands and very quickly my grunts of pleasure matched his in timing and volume. Finally with a cry Kurt climaxed sending jism shooting up inside me, I could have sworn that I felt each and every jet of jism he ejected but perhaps that was just my imagination.

Spent and exhausted he collapsed on top of me driving the air out of my lungs with a groan. Apologetic Kurt rolled over to one side dragging me with him until we were lying spooned together with his cock still buried in me. We laid like that for a while content to cuddle and enjoy the moment, I for one was certainly enjoying having my hole stuffed so continuously. Before long Kurt was ready to go again, remaining in this position we had a slower more sedate fuck but one that I was able to enjoy as I was free to back onto his cock as the mood took me. I thought that being his second go his climax would be less vigorous and noisy, but I was mistaken for I still got a punishing banging just prior to him sending yet more jism up me.

I made to move away but quickly found this impossible as his arm was firmly wrapped around my stomach refusing to let me go.

"Not so fast Danny boy, I haven't catered to your needs yet, I'll let you know when you can get up" he said making it clear that he was in control of the situation.

I didn't try very hard to resist, although my anal ring was beginning to get sore from all the polishing it was getting, it had been such a long time since I'd had such an energetic time in bed that I was content to lay where I was. Ten minutes later Kurt's cock was erect once more and making its presence felt inside me, however this time he had other plans for us.

He rolled onto his back and still impaled by his cock I was manoeuvred into a position where I was straddling his waist, facing him. While I rode up and down on his pole like a cowboy on a bucking bronco he took hold of my own cock and stroked it to erection. Having been pent up for so long it didn't take me long to cum sending my own jism flying across his stomach and onto his chest with an audible splat. My orgasm was made all the more intense by the cock inside me hitting my prostate every time I slid up and down it. My anal ring clenched spasmodically around his shaft which in turn sent Kurt over the edge as he too shot his third and final load up inside me within a minute of my orgasm.

Finally spent I was allowed to climb off him and with a loud wet slurp his cock slipped out of my stretched and very tired anus. Both exhausted we staggered into the shower room where we cleaned ourselves off all the while acting like teenagers on our first date (which I guess it was). By the end of my own shower I had to make an emergency visit to the toilet as a large quantity of jism was now ready to leave me, well what goes up must come down as they say.

Crossing the hallway back to Kurt's bedroom I could hear that the TV was still on with Logan and Wayne's voices talking over it. I just hoped that they hadn't heard too much of our lovemaking noises. I guessed I would find out in the morning if they had! Sleep came to me quickly and my last conscious thought was of how much I liked the way Kurt smelt when he was fresh out of the shower and how he held me in his arms beneath the duvet.

Chapter 3 – The morning after the night before

I woke with a start the following morning with the sun streaming in through the window blinds. It created bright stripes across the bed and opposing wall but it wasn't the bright light that had roused me from my slumber. I had felt a couple of greasy fingers explore between my cheeks sliding towards their target, no prizes for guessing where they were heading. Sure enough, having found my anus the hand the fingers belonged to spread my cheeks and I felt the familiar jolt of cold KY being spread all round my ring and inside.

Sighing contentedly I closed my eyes and pushed backwards onto the fingers exploring my anus. I heard Kurt chuckle behind me before the fingers withdrew only to be replaced by a now very familiar cockhead. Having been stretched so thoroughly the night before it took no time at all for me to swallow Kurt deep inside me with no discomfort. Held close against his body Kurt slowly and leisurely fucked me, I thought I'd died and gone to heaven! We were still in mid-fuck when there was a knock on the door and Logan stuck his head round the door.

"Jeez, you two aren't still shagging are you?" he asked with a grin on his face "Wasn't three times last night enough for you?! Kurt I just wanted to let you know that Ralph expects to see you this morning, if you know what I mean."

"Yeah yeah I get the message Logan, won't be long" Kurt replied without missing a stroke in his fucking of my arse.

"Okey dokey, see you guys for breakfast" Logan replied before closing the door on his exit.

"Does he always do that?" I asked.

"Do what?" Kurt asked upping the pace of his thrusts.

"You know, being so casual about... you know what I mean" I replied in between grunts as he hammered against my back door.

"Oh that. Of course, I've done the same thing in the past. We're very causal round here you know, we have no secrets, nor shame for that matter!" he informed me.

Boy did Kurt have stamina, it seemed like ages before I felt him first shudder and falter in his thrusts, then with a guttural growl he shot his jism into me. He held me briefly in a crushing embrace before whispering in my ear

"God, I just love fucking you. I wish we could stay here in bed all day but I've got a job to do and word has already got round."

"Got round? What do you mean?" I asked.

"Like I said we have no secrets. You can't fart in this business without someone hearing it. No doubt as soon as Wayne left here the jungle drums would have been beating and Ralph's message meant business before pleasure. That guy knows me too well!" Kurt chuckled as be planted a kiss on my shoulder.

I turned my body to return the kiss but Kurt was already pulling out of me and sliding out of bed. Before getting up I did allow myself the pleasure of watching Kurt's naked body sauntering out of the bedroom and into the bathroom. As for me the toilet was calling to me, I needed to pee and evacuate Kurt's latest little present, by the time I had finished in there I could hear the shower running and Kurt's slightly off-key voice singing "Bad Romance" by Lady Gaga. Smiling wryly to myself I thought that man's perfect in every way except for his voice, but I can live with that especially when he's got a body to die for!

Ten minutes later we had both showered and towelled each other dry, raced to get dressed and sat around the dining table before Logan had a chance to chase us up. He looked up in surprise from the newspaper he was reading and then down at his watch.

"Not bad, only five minutes late Kurt. Ralph will be impressed."

"Surely five minutes is bad?" I asked with the distinct impression that there was more to this than I knew about.

"No. Five minutes is good" Kurt informed me "I have been known to be more than an hour late for work and that was just because I overslept."

Over waffles and strong black coffee the three of us made small talk and planned for the day ahead. Both Kurt and Logan had to start work shortly and wouldn't finish until rally had closed for the day. Kurt told me he would drop me off home and then pick me up again later this evening. I tried to convince Kurt that I was happy to hang around at the rally if it was easier for him but he made it quite clear that he'd made the decision and that was that. This was the first time that I had experienced Kurt's alpha male assertiveness directed towards me and to my surprise I was aroused by it. So before I knew it I was once more riding pillion on Kurt's motorbike, holding on for dear life as he sped me home.

Standing on the pavement beside his bike I felt a little sad as I removed my helmet and stowed it away in the pannier. Insecurity had been gnawing away at my insides as I worried that this was going to be nothing more than an extended one night stand.

"Hey, why are you frowning?" Kurt asked as he removed his own helmet and hung it on his handlebar.

"You will be coming back to pick me up tonight won't you?" I blurted out without thinking.

"Ah is this what you've been fretting about ever since breakfast? You have my word. I will definitely be coming over after work to collect you, why wouldn't I?" he asked looking a little confused.

"Has it been that obvious? I'm just worried that I'll be nothing more than a one night stand, soon forgotten as you move onto another town. I like you, I like you very much" I admitted.

I felt my face flushing red at having made such a bold statement in a public place. Well, we were standing on the main high street after all, with shoppers passing by.

"Well you can stop worrying right now because I don't do one night stands. You're definitely not easy to forget, what with your handsome face and your gorgeous arse which I just want to fuck all the time. Now come here" he said in that authoritive tone I can't resist.

"What...." I went to say but was cut off as Kurt pulled me to him and kissed me passionately on the lips.

After a moment or so he released me and I took a breathless step back, almost knocking over a scowling elderly lady who muttered something under her breath as she walked on by. Kurt pulled on his helmet before assuring me once again that he'd call by after work and that he'd call me when he was leaving. With a wave of his hand he roared off down the main street leaving me feeling somewhat abandoned and alone.

Back to the real world I thought as I opened the door to my empty flat and heard the feint bleeping of my answer phone. Sighing I walked over to the machine, pressed the play button and listened to the increasingly concerned and irritated messages left by Perry and Lewis wanting to know why I had not been answering my mobile phone. Well it didn't ring I thought but then spotted the said phone abandoned on the windowsill, I must have left it behind in my hurry to get ready for my date the previous evening. Oops! Perhaps it was just as well considering the activities of the night for it would have been annoying to have been in mid-fuck with the phone ringing!

An hour later having changed into fresh clothing and poured myself an orange juice I picked the phone and dialled Perry's number first. He was relieved to hear my voice as he was genuinely worried about my sudden silence for we're always chatting or texting, but as the conversation went on he realised that I was not telling him everything. Sensing that there was gossip to be shared he insisted on meeting me in our favourite cafe for a coffee and debriefing. It was useless trying to argue with him and if I'm honest a little part of me wanted to tell him about the fact that I had pulled the guy he had raved about. I cut the conversation as I had to call Lewis too and repeat the conversation all over again with him, but knowing his opinion of Kurt I was a little more circumspect.

It was late lunchtime by the time we met up at out chosen cafe and as I munched on my bacon and cheese melt I recounted the tale of my date and in graphic details about what happened between the sheets. Lewis, ever the cautious one was horrified by the risks that I had taken in the name of adventure and pleaded with me to be more careful in the future. Perry on the other hand appeared to be more than a little envious. I think it was a combination of me getting the guy that he'd fancied and the amount of action I'd seen last night. I couldn't help but pull his leg and offered to set him up on a blind date as I was sure that there must be other single guys working with Kurt. Just for a moment I saw temper flare up as pride nearly got the better of him, but quickly putting a lid on it he laughed and said

"I can find my own talent but if Kurt has a twin brother then I might be interested."

"Well I think Logan is single and I guess you might like him, he seems like a nice guy. I'll find out tonight if he's gay shall I?" I replied in a carefully neutral tone so he didn't think I was winding him up.

"Are you serious? You're winding me up aren't you?" Perry asked full of suspicion.

"Absolutely not, I promise!" I said raising my hands in the air to emphasise the point.

"Well okay but don't make it sound like I'm a saddo or desperate, please" he said with a pained expression on his face.

"If I see Logan tonight I'll make discrete enquiries and give him your number. What you do from there is up to you" I replied waving to the waiter to gain his attention.

We split the bill three ways before doing some retail therapy in the shopping arcade. I wasn't that interested as my mind was largely focussed on Kurt wondering how his day was going and what he was doing, but I felt that it was only fair to my best mates to spend some time with them do what they enjoyed doing. As they trawled through the bargain rails of the department store I had to smile thinking how my perspective had changed in less than forty eight hours. Only last week we had done virtually the same activity with me leading the way, now I was taking a backseat while they fought for the best bargains. In the end I called it a day promising Lewis that I'd be careful and Perry that I would text him later with news on Logan. I raced home eager to get washed and ready for my second date with Kurt.

Chapter 4 – An invitation that's hard to refuse

At last my mobile phone rang, it was Kurt apologising for being slightly late (well half an hour to be precise but I wasn't going to point that out to him) and that he would be with me within fifteen minutes. I assured him that everything was cool and that I'd wait for him outside so that we could get straight off to wherever we were going. With a grunt of approval he hung up and I got my gear together, this time I remembered to put my mobile phone into my overnight bag so that I could text Perry later as promised.

Kurt must have been racing because I had only just locked my front door and stepped onto the main path when I heard the familiar roar of his bike's engine in the distance. Then before I knew it he had screeched to a halt next to me and pointed to the pannier where I was to stow my stuff having retrieved the spare helmet first. He didn't say a word to me until I was sitting behind him on the bike, helmeted and with my arms wrapped securely around his middle. Then the integral headphones activated with a bleep and I heard his deep masculine voice come through clearly. He told me that he'd bought the gear this afternoon and had paid for an express fitting which was why he had been running late. I assured him again that I was cool with things and just glad to be with him again, I then asked where we were going but he told me to leave the details to him and just enjoy the ride. So I did. I watched over his shoulder the scenery flashing past as we headed up the interstate and presumably to Lake George again. We were but not to the camp site as I expected, instead we veered off and drove into Lake George State Park. It was late evening and not surprisingly the park was largely empty except for a few dog walkers on the main grassy area. We rode past with no one taking any notice of us at all and continued deeper into the park until Kurt had found a suitably secluded area away from prying eyes.

Dismounting we stowed our helmets away and to my surprise Kurt retrieved a blanket and set up a regular picnic for us both. I stood there like a grinning idiot before sighing and saying

"I never knew you were such a romantic, I'm really touched by this" I said waving my hand in the direction of the picnic.

Laughing he replied "There's no such thing as a free lunch, there's something you've got to do before you can sit down and eat.

"Oh? What's that?" I asked but the answer was already clear from the Kurt's actions.

He was now standing directly in front of me with hands on hips and a big dirty grin and simply said "You know what you gotta do."

I sure did so with a grin matching his I sank down to my knees and with one hand unbuttoned his leather trousers and with the other unzipped his flies. With murmurs of encouragement from above I pulled his leathers down to his knees revealing that he had gone commando. His cock was already semi-erect and swung freely before my face getting harder by the second. Unfortunately for me he was not very fresh and I could smell a combination of leather, sweat and stale urine every time his cock swung past my nose. Naturally I was reluctant to get closer to it even though the sight of his huge cock made my mouth salivate. Perhaps he sensed this or it might just have been a power trip for him because without warning I felt a hand grasp the back of my head and guide it onto his cock.

Something clicked inside. I became a real slut as I opened my mouth wide and took his cock deep into my mouth totally ignoring the initially sour taste in my mouth. The taste quickly disappeared as my saliva washed it clean and I set about giving him an energetic blow job. With his ever present guiding hand I soon had his cock fully buried down my throat, somehow I managed not to gag as he fucked it with abandon. It helped to focus on the feel of his balls hitting my chin and the tickling sensation of his pubes against my lips each time he thrust forward. I wrapped my arms around him for support and placed each hand on his cheeks feeling his hard muscles with every move he made.

He would occasionally pull out completely, lift my chin and tell me what a good boy I was before ramming his cock back down my throat. All good things must come to an end however, and as I began to get cramp in my jaws for being held open for so long, I felt his body go into spasm. Then with his cock fully buried down my throat he shot load after load of his jism down into my stomach. Only when he had finished ejaculating did he release his hands from my head and pull his saliva coated cock from my mouth. Unable to resist I gave his cock head one last lick as I noticed a glob of jism had pooled at the end and threatened to fall to the ground. Well it was a shame to see it going to waste!

This move clearly pleased Kurt for he pulled me to my feet and told me yet again what a good boy I was and kissed me hard on the lips not caring if he could taste his own jism. It was as if the moment had passed, Kurt took a step backwards from me and pulled his leathers back up. I just stood there a little uncertain about what was happening but I needn't have worried for he simply sat down cross legged on the blanket and started to unpack the food. I joined him on the blanket and we hungrily ate the food in silence. It was only after most of the food had been wolfed down and we had repeatedly belched in typical male fashion that we grinned at each other and normal conversation resumed. We talked about anything and everything, ranging from past love affairs to awful jobs endured; our favourite films to places we wanted to visit. The gentleness and maturity Kurt displayed towards me at that point seemed to be in direct contrast of the hardened biker come fighter image I saw before me. I gave up trying to rationalise the differences and decided to enjoy the moment for what it was, a quiet picnic with a very horny butch guy who I was getting to know very intimately.

With a can of lager in one hand and the other hand wrapped around his waist I sat leaning contentedly against him taking in the vastness of the starry night time sky. The moon had just risen above the trees throwing its eerie sliver glow over us when I felt a shiver run down my spine in response to the coolness of the night time air. Kissing me tenderly on my forehead Kurt announced that it was time to make a move and proceeded to pack the picnic up and stowed everything into the bike's panniers. I felt a little disappointed that our time was up so soon but as I reached in for my helmet Kurt slapped my hand away telling me that he had a little treat in store for me. I knew better than to ask so I let him take me by the hand and off we walked further into the woods which got darker and darker as the moonlight was left behind.

We hadn't gone far when Kurt found an apparently suitable spot, just off a side path, where he stopped abruptly and pulled me to him. For several minutes he kissed me passionately, grinding his hips into mine in a deliberate attempt to arouse me. I felt his hands start to unfasten my jeans when without warning he froze and I felt his body stiffen in an instant. Putting a finger to my lips to silence me he remained rooted to the spot, moving just his head in the direction of a sound that only he could hear. I strained my ears and then I heard it, footsteps coming towards us along the path only feet away from us.

I felt fear take hold of me as I realised that there was more than one person, judging by the sound of the footsteps and the quiet voices discussing where their target may be hiding. What were they doing out here in the woods late at night and why along this less well used path? Suddenly there was a bright flash as a torch was switched on and its beam pierced through the gaps in the foliage. Thankfully the beam missed us and we remained hidden in the darkness. Taking slow and silent breaths we remained stationery waiting for the footsteps to recede into the distance, finally Kurt seemed satisfied that the coast was clear and indicated that we should make our way back to the bike. We walked briskly back the way we had come with me looking over my shoulder nervously for any sign that we were being followed. I was relieved when we reached the clearing where the bike was still standing just as we had left it.

My relief was short lived for as we crossed the clearing I heard a loud voice call out from the inky blackness.

"Oi Eddie! The fucking poofs are back! Come on let's get them!"

Kurt and I turned reflexively to face the source of the sound just in time to see three gangly skinhead youths burst out of the bushes running towards us with ugly sneers on their faces.

"Get behind me" I heard Kurt whisper to me.

Scared, I did as I was told, for I had never been in this situation before. Although I'd been teased and called names at school I had never been the target of a homophobic attack before.

"Ah how sweet!" the ring leader said "big butch bum boy protecting his little cocksucker. Won't do you no good though, you're both gonna get what you deserve."

"That's right, let's smash their pretty little faces in" said the one who had called out first.

By now they were circling us like marauding jackals, snarling and clenching their fists as they did so, moving in ever closer.

"Look guys" Kurt said amazingly casual "I don't know what your game is but if I were you I'd back off and leave us alone."

"Oh you would, would you?" the ring leader said mimicking Kurt's tone before continuing with "we saw you sickos with your little pre-picnic game. You make me sick" and he spat to emphasise his point.

I could see Kurt's temper coming up to the boil as his fists clenched and unclenched while shifting his weight from leg to leg. Unfortunately for the ring leader he interpreted that as a sign of weakness and took a step closer to us, a step too close as it turned out. Before anyone could react, Kurt's right fist lashed out striking the guy hard in the side of his face, then, almost simultaneously his left fist smashed into his unprotected stomach. The ring leader crumpled to the ground totally winded, writhing and groaning in pain.

Unfortunately this assault provoked the other two into launching their own attacks on us. Shouting in anger the smaller of the two flew at me, covering the ground between us in two strides. I've never been a fighter as I'm not very strong and my conscious brain didn't know what to do to defend myself. Thankfully my sub-consciousness did and immediately took control of my body. As my attacker came into range my right leg shot into the air and my foot made satisfying contact with his crutch, making his scream in pain as his bollocks were crushed between my toe cap and his thighs. He crashed to the ground, curling up into a foetal position he cupped his crown jewels with his hands and made strange mewling noises. Stunned at my success I looked round wondering what to do next. I was just in time to see Kurt land a knockout punch on the third and final attacker who fell unconscious to the ground.

My body started to tremble as the adrenalin rush subsided and I went into shock. I felt Kurt take hold of my elbow and push me towards his motorbike.

"Come on Danny" Kurt said to me "I need you to remain focused as we only have a couple of minutes before these brain-dead monkeys recover. If we hang around we will have lost the element of surprise and will have trouble on our hands."

As he said this one of the thugs raised his head and snarled in our direction as if to emphasise Kurt's statement. Fear jolted me into action so I quickly donned my crash helmet, climbed onto the bike and held on for dear life as Kurt revved the engine into life. As we sped off over the grass I could hear the skinheads shouting vengeance, I just hoped they didn't catch up with us or know where we were heading.

My nerves had calmed down by the time we arrived back at the trailer and Kurt acted as if nothing had happened as we dismounted the bike and stowed the helmets away. He held me at arms distance and gave me a searching look before asking me if I was okay, I nodded and gave a half smile. He nodded in approval before giving me quick hug and then led me by the hand into the trailer where Logan was once again sprawled out on the sofa watching a soccer match. I stood there half watching the game and half wondering how I was going to ask Logan if he wanted to go on a blind date with my friend Perry. I tried to make small talk with Logan but to be honest he was more interested in the match than talking to me and appeared a little relieved when Kurt got impatient and practically dragged me into the bathroom.

Locking the bathroom door behind us Kurt practically ripped my clothes off, well he would have if I hadn't co-operated by undoing the buttons and moving as quickly as he did! Pushing me into the shower he told me to turn it on and as I did so he stripped off leaving our clothes in a jumbled heap by the door. It was a tight but pleasurable squeeze in the shower, which was really only meant to be used by one person at a time. There is something highly erotic about soaping up a naked man's body while he is doing the same to you and in less than a minute we both had raging hard ons. As we stood underneath the stream of hot water Kurt held me close, rubbing our cocks together before whispering in my ear

"I want you."

"I want you too" I replied hoarsely trying not to cum there and then.

"Let's go to bed and I'll give you that treat I promised you earlier"

I raised my eyebrows in response before I set about rinsing the soap off us. Kurt was clearly impatient for once the stream of water had diminished to a trickle he pushed open the shower door, picked up the heap of clothes and strode off towards his bedroom without stopping to dry himself. Keen not to slip on the tile floor with wet feet I paused long enough to dry my feet before I too headed for the bedroom.

As I walked into the room the door slammed shut and I felt myself being manhandled. Pushed roughly backwards I lost my balance and fell spread eagled on top of the duvet. Before I could react I felt my ankles being gripped, then simultaneously lifted into the air and brought closer together. I looked down the length of my body in surprise to see Kurt sinking to his knees and sliding his hands down my legs until they were holding the backs of my thighs. He pushed my thighs closer to my torso and then buried his face between my spread cheeks. I giggled as his beard tickled my crack and then moaned in appreciation as his tongue found my sensitive anus. The tip of his tongue flicked and prodded all around the ring before pushing against my opening gently. Withdrawing momentarily it returned liberally applying saliva to my ring as it did so I could feel myself opening up welcoming him inside me.

"Good boy" he murmured half muffled by my cheeks "for that you win the main prize."

"Which is?" I asked.

"You're about to find out" he replied with a dirty grin on his face "pass me the KY."

I glanced over at the bedside cabinet he had nodded towards and with one hand picked up the half empty tube, unscrewed the top and passed it to him through my open legs. He took it without saying a word and with a firm squeeze applied it to my hole. As always the cold gel made my hole quiver in response before relaxing once again. I didn't have long to wait for my main prize, for Kurt quickly rose to his feet and crouched over me. To free up his hands I wrapped my arms around the back of my knees and pulled my legs back against my chest, exposing my backside still further. Then I felt the tip of his cockhead press against my hole and with barely a pause he pushed inside and slid all the way up only stopping when he was fully buried within me. I cried out in response to the sudden intrusion but he ignored me, for the alpha male in him seemed to be in control and my feelings were of no consequence.

Admittedly, I was hardly a virgin and I just loved my rectum being stretched by his huge cock so within a very short space of time I had forgotten the discomfort and was enjoying the impalement. He fucked me slowly with long smooth strokes of his cock, pulling out until just his cock head was inside me and then pushing back on up until he could go no further. In and out, in and out, over and over again, never speeding up or slowing down. This was so much different to the other fucks that I had enjoyed with him, a real head trip for me to see him looming over me in total control. He was doing just what he wanted and I loved it big time. I reached up and gently tweaked his nipples between my finger tips, he groaned in response and told me to keep doing it, so I did.

I don't know how long we carried on like this for time had become suspended for me until he simply stopped with his cock buried in me. I looked up at him just as he looked down at me and asked in a serious tone.

"Do you want to be my cub?"

I remembered what Kurt had said about it being a term of endearment. I interpreted it to mean in biker's term for a lover or boyfriend, obviously a junior which made sense as I was younger than him. As this was the second time he had used this term I felt confident that Kurt was serious about us being together. Happily I reached up and kissed him passionately before letting go I replied.

"Yes, I would love to be your cub."

"Are you absolutely sure about this?" Kurt asked deadly serious "Once you have agreed to be my cub there is no going back for either of us as far as I am concerned."

His intensity troubled me briefly but at the same time it thrilled me for no guy had ever wanted me this badly before, so with a slow nod of my head I reconfirmed that I wanted to be his cub. My answer clearly pleased him for Kurt grinned happily before he resumed fucking me, more vigorously this time and a lot more noisily. Until that is there was a bang on the door and Logan asked us to keep the noise down for he was trying to get some sleep! Kurt laughed and apologised before he covered my mouth with his hand and pounded away at my arse until with controlled grunts he shot his load of jism deep into my bowels followed seconds later by my own splattering over my chest.

Collapsing on top of me Kurt lay there slowly regaining his breath, before he carefully wiped us clean with some tissues he pulled out from a drawer. Exhausted by the day and the recent athletics we crawled beneath his duvet and drifted off to sleep in a tight embrace.

Chapter 5 – An introduction to the clan

Morning came all too soon. One moment I was dead to the world, the next I was wide awake as my ears tuned into Kurt's clock radio announcing the eight o'clock news. I lay there for a minute or two willing my body to move but I was just so comfortable and warm snuggled against Kurt's body. I went to close my eyes and drift off back to sleep when it suddenly dawned on me that today was Monday.

"Shit!" I groaned as I sat up in bed "I'm going to be late. I've got to be in work in half an hour!"

Kurt simply opened one eye, reached out with an arm and pulled me closer to him.

Then he whispered in my ear "call in sick."

"I can't, I don't get paid if I'm off sick" I replied trying to ignore his gentle nibbling of my ear lobe.

"Hey Danny, live a little and go with the flow" Kurt murmured as he kissed my neck "besides as you're now my cub it's up to me to provide for you."

"I can pay my own way, thanks, and I really do need to go into work" I insisted as I tried to extricate myself from his arms.

Kurt however had other ideas. Refusing to let go of me he rolled me onto my back before laying on top using just his elbows to support himself. He kissed me tenderly on the lips before looking me in the eye and said

"I'm being serious and I'm not going to take no for an answer. I said I'm going to take care of your every need whether it be emotional, sexual, financial or whatever. All I ask is that you trust me and let me lead the way. Have you already forgotten that you're my cub?"

I shook my head and gave myself up to his persuasive lips as they kissed their way slowly down my body and along my cock's increasingly erect shaft. Moments later I was rock hard and buried deep inside a hot tight throat, heaven!

Sometime later that morning having drifted off back to sleep after the exquisite blow job, I finally surfaced from our love nest. By now I was desperate for a pee and used this as an excuse to escape from his clutches. Before he could follow I quickly locked the bathroom door behind me and made good use of the toilet followed by a dash next door for a shower and shave. Over the noise of the shower I heard Kurt banging around in the kitchen area so breakfast was on its way much to my stomach's relief!

Having got dressed I sauntered into the lounge to see that Kurt had already made two mugs of strong black coffee and was busy toasting some bread. Sitting down on a sofa I sipped my coffee and watched him while he worked. I still had trouble believing that I had managed to bag myself such a handsome hunk of a man that was also good in bed. He wore just a black jockstrap, which somehow made him appear more naked than if he had actually been so. It contrasted with his white cheeks whose muscles tensed and flexed with his every move, drawing my eyes to them as if they were magnets. Dragging my eyes away from his backside I studied his tattoos in more detail. The ones on his back reminded me of a jungle scene, an intertwined mixture of black panthers and green foliage, starting just above his pelvis and running up his back as a narrow band before flaring out rapidly as it met his shoulder blades. On his right bicep there was a broad band in black with gothic script making it hard to read from this distance. Either side of the band were paw prints in keeping with the panther theme. On his left bicep was an intricate design of a bear riding a motorbike and the name "Honaw" beneath it in the same gothic script as on the other arm.

I was so engrossed that I didn't realise that Kurt had been talking to me, until he turned round and stood with hands on hips facing me and said in a loud voice.

"Hey! Earth calling Danny, anyone at home?"

"Uh? Oh sorry, I was miles away. What did you say?" I replied a little embarrassed.

"I was simply asking you what you wanted on your toast that was all" Kurt said with a grin on his face.

"Oh, I'll have it plain, just a little butter please. What's funny?" I asked.

"Nothing, I just love how you can go from white to bright red so quickly!" he laughed bringing over a plate stacked up with buttered toast.

Sitting down next to me on my left I was able to see clearly for the first time what the gothic script writing said on his arm – "Kurt cub of Dexter 1996". He caught my gaze and between mouthfuls of toast asked me if I liked his tattoos.

Nodding my head I replied "Yes, very much so. They are beautiful and of high quality, I can tell they weren't done in a typical back street tattoo parlour."

"Thank you. I must admit I am proud of them and you're right, they were done by a master tattooist. Our clan has long standing and close connection with him for he has done all of our clan tattoos" he said matter of factly.

Silently we ate our toast and sipped our coffees. I was so full of questions that I didn't know where to start, in the end I never asked them because I suddenly remembered about Perry and my promise to him.

"Kurt, I know this is going to sound an odd question but is Logan single?"

"Why do you ask?" Kurt replied frowning a little.

"Only because I promised Perry that I would see if I could arrange a blind date for him...." I trailed off seeing him deep in thought.

"Mmm it's not that simple" Kurt said between sips of coffee. "Yes, Logan is single and he's normally up for some man to man action but he rarely dates as a rule."

"You say 'normally', what do you mean?" I asked puzzled by his reply.

"Well for a start Logan is bisexual, he likes men and women in equal measure. His favourite scene is a threesome with a straight or bisexual couple where he can get to fuck both partners."

"Really?" I said without thinking.

"Oh yes, I've seen him in action before. That was one wild party we went to!" Kurt giggled at the memory.

"So why does he rarely date?" I asked pressing the point.

"Simply because he doesn't like being tied down and won't turn down an opportunity if it presents itself. So if Perry fancies having a fuck with Logan then I'm sure he'll be up for it but if he's looking for a relationship he may end up heartbroken." Kurt said as he collected up our empty plates.

"Okay, thanks for that info. Will you sound out Logan to see if he'd be interested before I speak to Perry and let him know what he's letting himself in for?" I asked following Kurt to the kitchen area and washed up the breakfast crockery.

To be honest I was procrastinating about phoning in sick but eventually I could put it off no longer and so with a shaking hand I dialled the store's number. It rang and rang but finally it was picked up the other end and I heard the familiar voice of my boss, the store manager. Having put on my best acting voice I persuaded him that I was too unwell to come into work today but that I should be able to come in tomorrow. On this last piece of information the relief in his voice was tangible and conversation ended on a good note.

It had been made a little easier to tell this little lie knowing that it would only be for the one day. It was Kurt's day off and then for the next few days he would be too busy with work to see me as the rally would have to be packed up before moving on to Ebensburg, Pennsylvania. This was why he was so keen for me to be with him today.

By now it was late morning and drinking yet another mug of coffee we sat next to each other on the doorstep of the trailer. Enjoying each other's close proximity the conversation changed from small talk to more personal disclosures in the form of what we would like in an ideal world. Kurt said that he wanted someone to love and giving me giving me a hug he said that he might just have found that person in me. Blushing a little at this remark I admitted that I had become bored with life and dreamed that some excitement might just happen before I get too old to enjoy it, plus of course finding that special person to love. I gave him a wink at this last bit and kissed him affectionately.

We savoured this loved up moment for as long as possible before our stomachs reminded us of the need to eat. As I made us both a round of ham salad sandwiches Kurt suggested that we pop back to my place so that I can pick up a change of clothing. I looked down at my rather crumpled and grubby clothes and agreed that this might be a good idea.

An hour later we were standing in front of my wardrobe with the doors wide open, I stood to one side while Kurt went through my clothes making it all too clear that he wasn't impressed by what he found. As he put my last shirt back into the wardrobe Kurt turned round and said

"To be honest I need to buy you a whole load of new clothes if you're going to be accepted by the clan members and integrate properly with the rally crew. These clothes just aren't up to the job."

I felt a little hurt by his comments and replied a little sulkily "I've always been one to keep up with high street fashions and they're all in good condition. I never keep old or tatty clothes as you can see."

Unrepentant Kurt nods his understanding before saying "Very shortly you will be moving in very different circles, you need clothes which are both more manly and also harder wearing."

Before I could respond he looked at his watch and announced "Come on, there's still time for some clothes shopping and as you know Glens Falls better than I do you can lead the way into town."

Still smarting a little from his remarks I made it clear that I was not really in the mood for retail therapy especially when I didn't need new clothes in my mind.

"Look, quit moaning" Kurt replied cheerfully "It's not going to cost you anything as I told you earlier, you're my cub so I will be looking after you. Now get a move on, we're leaving before it's too late."

Apparently the subject was now closed as he simply turned on his heels and walked out through my front door. The idea that I wouldn't be paying for this shopping spree cheered me up no end and I was even able to forgive him for saying that my clothes weren't manly! By the time I had locked my door and caught up with him I was smiling in anticipation of spending his money.

The first shop we called into was just a couple of blocks down the road from where I lived, "Halls Sportsworld" which did pretty much what it said on the label. It sold every sports related item you could imagine in a building which appeared bigger on the inside than it did from outside. The owner had in fact bought a number of properties in the same block over the years and gradually connected them to one another. Not being a particularly athletic person I had never had cause to use the shop, so being a new to the place I couldn't believe how big the shop was, it was like an Aladdin's cave (with treasure being replaced by clothes). Kurt quickly scanned the place before with shopping trolley at hand he selected a dozen pairs of jock straps, all black, to contrast with my pale skin so he said. I questioned the fact he hadn't checked my waist size, only to be told that he had, over the weekend in fact, by looking in my boxer shorts. Sneaky beggar! I thought to myself, I wonder if he sniffed them too. No, no, get that thought out of my head, right now! Next to be put in the trolley were several pairs of jogging bottoms with matching tops and flimsy running shorts. At the checkout I nearly had a fit when I saw the total cost but Kurt didn't bat an eyelid, he simply paid by credit card and thanked the young cashier with a beaming smile.

Next stop was "Denman's Clothing Store" which was a good ten minute walk across town in a purpose built unit specialising in outdoor clothing and work wear. Kurt got down to business immediately, armed with shopping trolley he quickly filled it with pairs of jeans, walking boots, running shoes and a couple of padded jackets. I knew the bill was going to be even bigger than the previous one, feeling a little uncomfortable I couldn't help but ask him if he would like me to pay towards it. His frown was enough to silence me and I let the matter drop. Kurt seemed satisfied with his purchases so laden down with bags we retraced our steps back to my home.

Dumping the bags on my bed I invited Kurt to stay a while for a well deserved drink. But with a shake of his head he declined saying that he needed to get back to the trailer and catch up with some chores. Feeling a little crestfallen I nodded my understanding, gave him a heartfelt hug and said

"Thank you for buying all those clothes for me, it's more than I was expecting."

"You're more than welcome" Kurt assured me returning the hug "and I look forward to seeing you wearing them."

With a final lingering kiss and a squeeze of my crutch he was gone, disappearing down the stairs and onto his bike parked outside. From the window I watched him roar off down the road disappearing in a cloud of dust. I sighed to myself having realised how empty my home now felt, but there was no use dwelling on the matter for Kurt had a job to do and so did I, well for the rest this week at least.

Later that evening as I got ready for bed my mobile buzzed, Kurt had sent me a text. Reading it I smiled to myself for he was missing me as I was him, not only that he had spoken to Logan and as he had predicted Logan was up for drink or two with Perry. Kurt included Logan's mobile number for me to pass on to Perry. I replied wishing him good night and thanked him for speaking to Logan for me.

The next four days dragged slowly past, each one following much the same routine. I'd get up in the morning, have a shower, eat my breakfast and text Kurt a short message before starting work at 8:30am on the dot. I kept up the pretence that I had been sick over the weekend and on Monday but was now better and enjoying being back at work (mmm not so sure about that last statement). Then between 1:00pm and 2:00pm I would meet up with Perry and Lewis for lunch at a little diner off the high street.

The first lunchtime we met I was grilled by both of them about what happened over Sunday evening and Monday. In a hushed voice so the other diners around me couldn't hear I described in great detail our antics over in the park, between the sheets and the clothes shopping yesterday. Lewis was still very much against Kurt because he simply doesn't like the macho alpha male types plus he thought Kurt is too old for me. I didn't take his criticism of Kurt personally because we're such good mates and I know that he only had my best interests at heart, so we agreed to differ over the man in question. Perry was a different matter, although he had some reservations about Kurt's nature he appeared to have been turned on by my narrative judging by his fidgeting. When Lewis went to relieve himself in the gent's toilets I passed to Perry Logan's mobile number and warned him about Logan's reputation. Perry thought for a moment before tucking the piece of paper into his wallet and grinning broadly he announced that shagging a male tart appealed to him no end!

After lunch I would return to work wishing the afternoon away before going home feeling lonely and at a loose end. While I prepared my evening meal I would call Kurt, despite the lengthy conversations and me telling him how much I missed him he would not take my bait about coming over. Instead he simply chuckled and told me to be patient until the weekend as he would have a treat in store for me. Then one evening he told me, well technically he asked me but I knew that he wasn't going to take no for an answer, to take next week off as annual leave. I asked him why as this was a bit short notice. All Kurt would say was that I would enjoy myself and get a taste of things to come if I was going to be a part of Kurt's life.

So the following morning having called in a few favours I persuaded my manager to allow me the following week off, he wasn't happy but felt compelled to say yes as I have always helped him out in the past.

Friday night finally arrived and as I walked in through my front door my phone rang, it was Kurt informing me that he was running late at work and wanted me to drive over with my new clothes and wait for him at his trailer. Thankfully I'd been lazy and left my new clothes in the store's bags so it was a simple matter to transfer them to the boot of my car! I was a little disappointed that he was still working but at least if I had to drive over to him I didn't have to wait here bored and lonely. So wasting no time I quickly showered and changed out of my works clothes before loading up my car and driving up to Lake George.

I parked the car in front of the trailer and saw that I was the first to arrive as Kurt's bike was nowhere to be seen. To my surprise I found the front door unlocked as I tried the handle. I called out a hello but no one responded so I went on in, dumped my bags on Kurt's bed and made myself at home.

Half an hour later Kurt walked in with a large paper bag in his arms followed by three other guys close behind. I stood up a little nervously as Kurt introduced me to them in turn. The oldest man was in his seventies, complete with a thick mop of white hair and matching beard. He went by the name of Owen Honaw and appeared to be in charge. The other two were in their fifties, looked quite similar in the fact they had close cropped salt and pepper hair with short tidy beards. Their names were Ralph Honaw and Dexter Honaw. With hands shaken and greetings completed we sat round the dining table while Kurt served up a feast from a local Chinese takeaway.

Over the meal the three newcomers gently quizzed me over my past, my jobs, my likes and dislikes, my plans for the future and my relationship with Kurt. However it was not one sided as I questioned them in return. I was curious about their common surname, are they all related? Owen explained that not one of them were biologically related, the name "Honaw" signified their membership of an exclusive clan (group). Membership was by invitation only and once accepted into the clan leaving is not an option.

To demonstrate this fact all four men rolled up their sleeves to reveal their right biceps. Each one had a tattoo identical to the one round Kurt's arm and on close inspection each had a similar message. Dexter's read "Dexter cub of Owen 1980", Ralph's read "Ralph cub of Harvey 1981" and Owen's "Owen cub of Wilson 1961". I finally understood why Kurt kept referring to me as his cub.

I could not help but look over at him and grin before asking "So will I be able to wear a similar tattoo if Kurt and I get it together?"

Owen replied in a friendly but authoritive tone "Wearing the tattoo isn't just about you loving Kurt. It also depends on you having the right attitude and sense of loyalty to the clan."

A little puzzled by this statement, I asked for clarification. Owen glanced at Kurt, who simply nodded in response before throwing me a wink.

"Okay, it's like this" Owen explained "if you seriously want to be part of Kurt's life then you will have to join the Honaw clan and assume the responsibilities that go with it. Such as living with and working for the clan, just as we have all done since the day we joined."

I nodded in response as I continued eating the remainder of my meal, appearing calm on the outside but my mind was frantically processing Owen's statement and the implications it had for me if I wanted to be with Kurt for the long term.

Once everybody had finished eating we quickly cleared the table and sat in the lounge where the probing questions started again. This time they focussed on my attitude to work, social situations and problem solving. Seemingly satisfied with my answers they turned their attention to Kurt and asked what clothing he had bought for me. Kurt started to explain then he obviously decided that it was easier to show them so barely pausing for breath he asked me to fetch the bags from the bedroom.

I jumped up eager to show that I had the right attitude and willing to follow Kurt's requests. I returned laden down with the bags and placed them on the dining room table before asking which item they wanted to see first.

"Not so fast Danny" Kurt replied with a straight face "first I want you to strip naked as you will have to model the clothes before the clan will give them their blessing."

I was stunned by his request but having looked at their expressions I realised that this was another test for me. So with a smile I simply replied "sure" and as casually as possible removed my clothes until I was standing before them stark bollock naked. I was then told to do a twirl so that they could have an all round view, which I did to sounds of approval.

Then one article at a time, I tried on all the clothing until I was standing fully clothed in my new gear and just a little irritated by Kurt's smug expression as Owen approved his purchases. My irritation was quickly forgotten when Owen looked over at me and told me to strip naked again as there was something he wanted to check. Sighing to myself I removed my clothes and stood before him as indicated with my hands clasped behind my back. Owen reached out and fondled my tackle until I was erect, he complimented me on my size before telling me to turn round and bend over at the waist. I blushed red with embarrassment but did as I was told, I felt a finger exploring my crack before it pushed its way past my ring and up into my rectum. It stayed there for a minute or two feeling its way around before withdrawing.

Owen then informed me that I was free to get dressed in my old clothes again and that as I would be living with Kurt that I should tidy my new clothes away in his wardrobe and chest of drawers. This was a poorly disguised excuse to get me out of the way so that they could discuss matters without me being present. I played along with the game and did as I was instructed. While in the bedroom I could not help but overhear Owen say to Kurt that I was too hairy and too tight to be seriously considered a cub. They were giving him (Kurt) one week to bring me up to an acceptable standard before they would reassess my potential again.

Not for the first time tonight I was confused by what they meant and if I was being honest, just a little hurt considering that I had done everything that had been asked of me. However I kept my feelings hidden and returned to the lounge pretending that I hadn't heard their conversation. I promised myself that later when we were alone I would get Kurt to explain what Owen had meant.

The evening continued very sociably as if the previous half an hour had never happened. It became apparent to me that the motorcycle rally would be packing up tomorrow and moving on to the next site - Ebensburg, Pennsylvania. Kurt made it quite clear that he expected me to join them and of course stay with him. So that was his plan I thought to myself, now I wonder what was the treat that he had in store for me?

Chapter 6 – The tattoo parlour

It was late that night by the time the three oldies left but Kurt had no intentions of going to bed, instead he wanted to go for a walk down by the lake. So with jackets on, for the night was chilly, we strolled down to the water front and along the lake shore holding hands. Once out of view from the camp site and other houses, Kurt stopped and held me close to him, then he told me that he'd fallen in love with me and hoped that I felt the same way too. I kissed him gently on the lips before I confirmed that I did and how happy I was now that I knew we felt the same way about each other.

Kurt's smile faltered as he looked away from me as if he was trying to find the right words to say to me.

"Hey, what's up?" I asked feeling that something serious was about to be said.

"Oh, it's just this clan business stuff. I need to tell you some things about it before we go much further but I don't want to say it the wrong way and scare you off" he replied looking distinctly troubled.

"Well you love me and I love you. You've asked me to trust you and I do. So please just be honest with me, how bad can it be? I'm not going anywhere I promise" I said looking deep into his eyes.

"Okay, here goes then" he said taking a deep breath "there are five rules of clan membership which cubs must obey if they want to join the clan."

"Go on" I said nodding encouragement.

"One, the cub has to be invited into the clan. Two, the cub has to pass the assessment and initiation rites before he can be accepted into the clan. Three, the cub has to remain faithful and loyal to his bear (that's me) all the time he's a cub. Four, the cub will obey all requests made and instructions given by his bear or any other clan member. Finally, number five, once accepted into the clan the cub is unable to leave, ever. So are you still interested?" Kurt asked holding my hands in a vice-like grip, as if to prevent me from running away.

Wincing slightly from the pressure I replied "If it means a life of adventure and being with you, then the answer is a definite yes."

Kurt was clearly relieved by my response and said "Excellent! In that case we need an early night as there are loads of things to be sorted out along with the normal day job, let's go."

The walk was over and within minutes we were back in the trailer shedding our clothes for a quick shower. I noticed that Logan was still nowhere to be seen and mentioned this to Kurt. Laughing as he towelled himself dry he told me Logan was unlikely to return tonight as he had arranged to meet Perry and by the sound of it he was planning to stay over at Perry's to give us some space for the night. Ah, I thought to myself, what's the betting that it was no coincidence that Owen, Ralph and Dexter called by on the same night that Logan had made himself scarce.

Back in our bedroom I crawled into bed only to find myself being pulled backwards with a "not so fast young man!" from Kurt. I looked over my shoulder to see Kurt retrieving the tube of KY from the bedside cabinet and lubing up his erection. No prizes for guessing what was coming! Always up for sex with Kurt I obediently positioned myself for easy access and reaching behind me I spread my cheeks apart.

"That's what I like to see, my cub keen to take my cock up his arse!" Kurt announced and slapped me on my backside.

"Ouch!" I cried in surprise to the stinging slap.

Before I could react Kurt had shoved his cock straight up me in one hard thrust, only coming to a halt when he was fully buried inside.

"Jeez Kurt! Go steady!" I cried out again "that hurts!"

"You'll get used to it young cub, your arse is going to see a whole lot more action very soon. My little cock here is going to be your best friend believe me and you won't want to be parted from it" he replied as he started to fuck me.

"I already love being fucked by you, but please go a little steady to start off with, just enough to get used to the intrusion" I grunted between thrusts.

"Like I said my cock will be a piece of cake for you before much longer, so you'd better get used to it now" he growled.

He placed a hand over my mouth effectively silencing me as he continued to pound my hole. Despite my initial misgivings and discomfort I really got into this scene. Being restrained and treated roughly had never been my thing but with Kurt it was a different matter. By the time he shot his load up me we were like two rutting beasts, just as well Logan was out otherwise he'd have been knocking on our door telling us to keep the noise down!

Exhausted from the bedroom athletics it didn't take Kurt long to fall asleep, whereas I lay there for what seemed like hours holding him close to me while I mulled over this evening's events and conversations. Eventually I drifted off into a restless sleep dreaming of being lost in a forest whilst unseen menacing animals stalked me roaring in the darkness.

I awoke late the following morning to find that I was alone in bed and Kurt nowhere in sight. Slipping on a pair of boxer shorts and a T-shirt I stepped outside the trailer and onto the still dew-damp grass. Taking deep breaths of fresh air I looked around me, it was then that I saw Kurt in the distance deep in conversation on his mobile phone. Not wanting to distract him I climbed back into the trailer and made myself some breakfast while I waited for Kurt to return.

Kurt returned a little while later with a distinctly satisfied look on his face and a bounce in his step. He strode over to where I was sitting and kissed me on the top of the head before saying

"Good morning, nice to see you're up and around – at last!"

"Cheeky beggar" I replied in mock indignation "I've been up at least half an hour."

"Well now that you are, and you've had breakfast" he said looking over at the bowl I had left unwashed in the kitchen sink "it's time for you to start your exercise regime."

"Eh? Just because I haven't washed up my cereal bowl?"

"Of course not" Kurt replied snorting "I expect you'll do that in any case. In consultation with the Owen I have devised an exercise regime designed to increase your fitness and strengthen your body."

"What's wrong with me as I am?" I asked looking down at my body.

"Nothing as far as I'm concerned" Kurt assured me placing a hand on my shoulder giving it a squeeze.

"So.....?" I asked pushing for an explanation.

"Owen is concerned that you will get injured in our line of work if you don't and if I'm honest I agree with him" he replied handing me a sheet of paper with a list of exercises on it.

I carefully read the instructions so that I understood what was required of me and was still reading them when Kurt interrupted me by saying

"I have to go in a minute to oversee the final clearance of the rally site, while I'm gone I want you to change into your running gear and do a lap of the camp site before doing today's exercises."

I was slightly irritated by Kurt's presumption and went to say something but having seen his expression I kept my peace and went to get changed. As I left the room I caught out of the corner of my eye Kurt smiling in satisfaction.

I returned a few minutes later having donned my running gear to find Logan and Kurt sitting together on the sofa talking quietly. As I walked into the room they both looked up but carried on talking with the occasional glance in my direction. Un-nerved by this strange behaviour I announced that I was off to do my run and made for the doorway.

"When you get back and have done your exercises" Kurt called out "make sure that you have a shower. I want you to wear your jogging bottoms and top but don't wear anything underneath, understand?"

"Yes Sir!" I said saluting and clicking my heels together.

I grinned to myself wondering if I was on a promise, well I had been a good boy and obeyed Kurt's every command!

So off I went on my run around the camp site happy in my assumption, I wasn't quite so cheerful by the time I got back to base and done seemingly endless squat jumps, press ups, ham string stretches and step ups. In fact the term knackered springs to mind! Exhausted I sat on the doorstep for a few minutes to get my breath back and let the heat from my body dissipate naturally. I certainly didn't need to be reminded about taking a shower for I could tell the deodorant I had put on earlier had long since worn off. I was only too pleased to stand under the hot stream of water easing my tired muscles.

Refreshed and smelling sweeter I dressed in the jogging bottoms and top I had left out on the bed before my run. I was just putting my socks and trainers on when Kurt returned. He poured us two glasses of cold orange juice from the fridge and together we sat on the door steps like I had half an hour ago. With one arm casually draped over my shoulder he pulled me against his body while he told me about how the trailer was going to be towed to the next site this afternoon by Logan using one of the clan's trucks. Apparently I would be driving the two of us there in my car with Kurt's bike stowed away in the truck with Logan.

By now I was starving so before we set off we wolfed down a couple of rounds of sandwiches and then packed my car up with essentials for our drive down to Ebensburg. As Kurt locked the trailer door behind us I took one last look around the camp site, something told me that I wouldn't be coming back here any time soon. Catching my expression Kurt asked if I was okay, I just smiled and nodded before climbing in behind the steering wheel and turned the ignition on.

Having filled my tank up with gas, we left Lake George and drove south along the Interstate 87. It was going to be a long drive, according to the route finder it would take over seven hours to reach Ebensurg, Pennsylvania and that wasn't allowing for convenience breaks. I was a little nervous because I've never driven so far in my life but Kurt didn't seem to think anything of it. For the next hour he regaled me with tales of his adventures while touring with the Honaw clan around the States. I gathered that the clan's rallies were held virtually continuously from spring until autumn with only the winter months for a break. We were just about to bypass Albany when Kurt suddenly came to life and asked me to leave the Interstate and turn right into Colonie.

I followed his instructions until we stopped outside a pretty ordinary looking shop, but appearances can be deceptive and as we stepped inside I realised that this was no ordinary shop at all. Every wall was covered from floor to ceiling with photographs of men and women decorated with tattoos. No prizes for guessing this was a tattoo parlour. I glanced at Kurt in surprise. He smiled before reminding me that when I have been accepted into the clan I will need to get some tattoos done so there's no time like the present to think about suitable designs. With that the proprietor appeared from the back of the shop, recognising Kurt he strode over to us giving Kurt a big bear hug and a slap on the back. With me he smiled and shook my hand vigorously.

"Well gentleman. Long time no see! How are you?" the tattooist asked addressing the question to Kurt.

"Very well thanks. Danny, this is Levi, Levi this is my cub Danny" Kurt said formally introducing us.

"Ah.... cub eh? I never thought I'd see the day when you, Kurt, would want to settle down. I guess you two are here to discuss designs amongst other things?" Levi said scratching his chin thoughtfully.

"Got it in one my friend" Kurt replied.

Levi didn't reply, instead he sauntered over to the door, dropped the catch and put up the closed sign before disappearing out the back again. Within a minute he returned with camera in hand and quite casually asked me to remove my clothes. I looked at Kurt for guidance who simply nodded his head, so not for the first time since meeting Kurt I was stripping for an audience. This can't have been a chance visitation, for Kurt had instructed me to wear minimal clothing presumably for just this situation.

I quickly removed my trainers and socks handing them to Kurt along with my jogging top and finally my jogging bottoms. I stood there stark naked and motionless while Levi circled studying me with the critical eye of an artist. Kurt put my clothes on a shelf behind the shop counter for safekeeping before joining Levi and together they quietly discussed aspects of my body structure. Levi then asked me to stand in various poses while he photographed me, explaining as he did so that every pose accentuated different groups of muscles. Finally satisfied that he had all the images necessary he led us through the door at the rear of the shop. I glanced longingly at my clothes but neither Kurt nor Levi made any reference to them so I assumed that I was to remain naked.

The room we entered appeared to be a cross between a living room and an artist's workshop, Levi invited us to sit down on the two available chairs while he made us coffee. Then for the next hour or so the three of us discussed designs that appealed to both Kurt and me. I had assumed that it would have to be identical to Kurt's but no, I was given free rein as long as they thought it suitably masculine. I have always been a fan of Greek mythology and reading alternative histories, so with a grin I explained want I had in mind.

On my back I wanted Medusa, the hideous Gorgon to be crouching victorious over the slain figure of Perseus. In a reversal of the traditional version, Perseus is killed by Medusa before he has a chance to defend himself. She is triumphantly holding his decapitated head high in one hand while with the other she supports herself with the bloody sword that killed Perseus. Her snake-like hair appears agitated and her bat-like wings are outspread reaching towards my shoulders. She wears a white toga in contrast to Perseus' naked body. His headless torso lays with a hand outstretched to the viewer and a nearby circular shield. Around the edge of the shield was the message "History is littered with fallen heroes". Then on my left bicep I wanted a ring of matching width to my "cub of" tattoo which will be of two intertwined snakes bordered by Greek style motifs.

When I had finished describing my design Kurt was silent and gave me a thoughtful look, then shook his head. Levi however seemed excited by the description and totally oblivious to Kurt's silence. He promised to make a start on the artwork tomorrow.

"Don't you approve of my choice?" I asked Kurt.

"It's not that I don't approve" Kurt replied carefully "rather, I'm not sure what message your tattoo is trying to convey. But hey, it's your choice, just be aware that once you've been inked it's there forever."

"Okay" I said nodding "that's fine, the meaning will come to you I'm sure. It will send a strong message when people see it and visually impressive, just like yours."

"Well, it will certainly be eye-catching that's for sure" Kurt agreed "I never realised that you were so blood thirsty."

"I'm not, it's just a simple reversal of a traditional legend along with a warning against vanity, but that is all I'm going to say on the subject. You will have to work the rest out for yourself" I declared with a slightly smug tone to my voice.

Levi seemed amused by our banter and told Kurt that he was going to have his work cut out with me. I bowed to Levi interpreting his statement to be a compliment.

Kurt thought otherwise because he said "No, I don't think so, he's coming along quite nicely in his training. Talking of which, time is getting on so let's get on with the next item on the agenda."

"Right you are" Levi nodded "let's move upstairs then."

Levi, closely followed by me and Kurt bringing up the rear, led the way up the stairs and into what would have been the front bedroom. I was shocked to see that it had been converted into what looked like a cross between a massage parlour and a doctor's surgery. Levi opened a drawer in a glass fronted cabinet and took out what appeared to be a cigarette. He lit it before handing it to me with instructions to smoke the whole joint.

Don't get me wrong, I'm not a prude and I've smoked the odd spliff or two but this was like nothing I've ever smoked before. To start off with it was strong and coarse, nearly making me choke to death for the first couple of drags, but then I became accustomed to it and it wasn't long before the effects started to present themselves. I was high as a kite, didn't care about anything and then slowly I started to feel tired as if I had been given a sedative. Kurt wavered in and out of focus; a hand reached out to me and guided me to the massage couch. Gratefully I climbed on to it and sprawled out before losing consciousness.

I dreamt of being a spit-roast pig over a fire being slowly turned by an unseen hand whenever the heat got too intense. Before long the pain became unbearable and I surfaced from my drug induced stupor, just in time to feel a stinging pain run down the back of my leg.

"Ah! That hurts!" I cried looking over my shoulder.

I was stunned to see Levi whipping off another waxing strip from my leg leaving a red stripe behind and ginger hairs stuck in the wax.

"Jeez…. what are you two doing to me?" I groaned and shifted my leg away from Levi.

Levi pulled my leg back and smeared more wax onto my calf before laying material strips on my leg before the wax solidified. I braced against the inevitable pain, as Levi took hold of the next strip Kurt crouched down beside me and coughed into my ear temporarily distracting me before he offered words of encouragement. I asked him between gasps of pain why I was being subjected to this agonising torture.

Kurt stroked my face tenderly before replying "No cub is permitted to have body hair. That is a privilege for bears in the clan. I too had to go through this ordeal when I was a cub but as you can see from my body my hair grew back normally. Once you have passed the assessment and initiation rite you will be allowed to re-grow your hair."

I nodded my understanding and gritted my teeth while Levi finished waxing my leg. Fortunately for me this was the last part of my body to be waxed as the more sensitive parts of my body had already been done while I was unconscious! My whole body felt it was on fire and it hurt to move any part of it. I was on the brink of crying when I felt a jolt of cold cream being drizzled all over my back and then hands expertly massaging the cream into my skin. It was bliss, for the cream quickly cooled the burning until it felt nothing more than mild sunburn. I sighed in contentment as my arms, back, legs, chest and tackle all received the cooling treatment. The last part to be addressed was my bum and as Kurt did his best to distract me I quickly realised why.

Levi poured copious amounts of the cream over my cheeks and along my crack, then with one hand he reached under me and pulled my cock and balls until they were lying exposed between my outspread thighs. He continued to massage them until I had a raging hard on, then more lightly to maintain my arousal before with his other hand he turned his attention to my arse. First he massaged the cream into my cheeks and then smeared the cream along my crack towards my anus. Instinctively I raised by hips to give him better access which only served to make Kurt chuckle and Levi comment about my willingness. All I could do was murmur in contentment, even more so when a finger pushed inside me and proceeded to smear the cream around inside my rectum. It was a strange sensation for it both cooled my insides and also relaxed my ring at the same time. A second finger joined the first and then a third, the three of them slowly and gently made swirling motions corkscrewing in and out of me. Levi tried to insert a fourth finger but my anus was fully stretched at three and wouldn't let it in. He made no comment and simply went back to fucking me with the three fingers which was just fine by me. Now he upped the tempo with his other hand and wanked me off until with a cry I shot jet after jet of thick jism all over the black PVC massage table. I could feel my ring spasm and clamp hard down on his fingers, effectively pushing them out as I did so.

As I came to from my orgasm I felt rather self-conscious out the mess I had made on the couch but Levi didn't seem put out in the slightest. He simply wiped the PVC clean with some tissues and helped me to sit upright. He then guided me out of the room and along the corridor and into what proved to be a bathroom.

"Danny, why don't you have a nice warm shower, take your time, get yourself clean and then join us down stairs. Oh, there's a fresh towel for you to use and when you do come down you're free to get dressed again" Levi informed me with a smile.

"Thanks Levi, I think a shower is just the thing I need right now" I said sincerely for by now I felt quite greasy from the cream that covered me from the neck downwards.

The door closed behind me, momentarily plunging me into darkness until I remembered where the light chord was and pulled it. The bright white neon light flashed on revealing multiple images of me everywhere I looked. Confused for a moment I quickly realised that each of the four walls had been covered from floor to ceiling in mirrors. It gave me an ideal opportunity to see what the waxing had done to me. The only hair remaining on me was now on my head and face, everywhere else was baby smooth and totally hairless. Gone was my ginger bush and chest hair! On the positive side it did make my cock look bigger being so exposed now, and being able to see every part of my body I thought how much I looked like a marble statue. The only difference was that I could move, which I did finally in the direction of the glass shower cubicle. Once the water had heated up I stepped inside to enjoy a long and luxurious hot shower.

Feeling clean and refreshed I turned the shower off, towelled myself dry and made my way along the corridor towards the staircase. It was silent upstairs so I presumed that the other two were by now waiting for me in the shop, descending the steps two at a time I was keen to get dressed again as it was distinctly chilly compared to the nice warm shower. The shop was empty when I got there so I retrieved my clothes and quickly got dressed before I went to search for the missing men. Stepping into the lounge come art room I could hear them talking quietly through a doorway that I hadn't noticed before.

Following the sound of their voices I walked into the room just in time to hear Levi say to Kurt

".... there is a whole lot of stretching to be done before he will be anywhere near ready."

I was about to ask what they were talking about when I was struck dumb by the contents of this hidden room. For lined up on shelves in front of me we dildos and butt plugs of all shapes and sizes plus dozens of cans of Crisco, again of various sizes. Along another wall stood enema equipment and butt machines, on another wall stood rails holding leather clothes and apparatus.

"Oh my God...." I muttered to myself.

Well no one else was taking any notice of me, that's for sure. Kurt was in deep discussion with Levi, who from time to time took a butt plug or dildo from the shelf and put it into a large black holdall bag. The dildos ranged in size from life size up to huge ones as big as a fire extinguisher! The butt plugs also ranged from small up to huge and I was alarmed to see that Levi had selected half a dozen dildos and the same again of butt plugs covering the whole spectrum of sizes. Once they were happy with the selection Kurt also selected an enema kit along with two large tins of Crisco.

I stood in the doorway feeling more than a little irritated that I hadn't been consulted once during the selection process, not that I would have known what I was looking for but that's beside the point. It didn't help that I was still a little sore from the waxing session and I wondered to myself if I had become involved with a madman. After Kurt paid for the items we bid Levi goodbye until after the initiation rites when I would be back to have the tattoos put on my back and arms. I was just as pleasant with Levi as I had been when we first met but with Kurt I was more distant and cool. I drove my car and followed directions given to me in a moody silence.

Kurt must have noticed the change in me but never said anything or acknowledged it until that is we pulled off the Interstate highway and stopped at a diner to eat. He ordered a meal for the two of us and led the way to a quiet spot where he asked me what was up and why had I become so moody?

It was like a dam bursting and in one rush I told him all about my concerns, the pain I had endured with the waxing and why do I have to go through all of this if it's just going to be the two of us?

"I promise, cross my heart and hope to die" Kurt said in a reassuring tone "that once you have become part of the clan it really will be just the two of us. In the mean time I have been tasked with getting you ready for the assessment and initiation so that you can pass with flying colours."

I took hold of his hand, not caring if anyone saw us and asked "But why an initiation? Why me?"

"Everyone goes through the same process" he replied "including me and if it's any consolation I asked the same questions myself and got the same answers too! Would it make you feel more relaxed about the whole thing if perhaps Dexter and I demonstrate what will happen during the assessment and initiation?"

I thought for a moment, nodded and replied "I think that would help no end, at least I would have an idea about what to expect."

That settled the matter, just in time for the waitress shortly after brought the food over and we ate in a comfortable silence content to simply eat the meal in front of us. I felt better in myself as Kurt appeared to be on the level with me and I felt I could trust him once more. The day was getting late and we still had an hour or so to travel so we wasted no time in driving on once the food had been eaten and paid for. While I drove Kurt called Dexter on his mobile phone and told him about our conversation in the diner and what we had agreed. The call went well judging by Kurt's expression as he hung up.

Chapter 7 – The training begins

We finally arrived at the newly established camp site at Ebensburg where there was (including ours) a total of eight trailers arranged in a square with a small enclosed green in the centre. A great deal of activity was still going on as everyone was busy setting up base and making themselves at home. We joined in the frantic activity for we had plenty to do ourselves before we could think about going to bed.

It was very late at night when Owen, the most senior clan member, called a clan meeting and everyone (approximately thirty in total) gathered in the central square forming a circle around Owen. He welcomed everybody and said that he was glad everyone had arrived safely after the drive down to the new site. He then asked for any guy applying for clan membership to step forward. I stepped into the ring along with three others guys, all of us around the same age, and we eyed each other nervously as we stood next to Owen. He put us at ease with a couple of clan jokes before he explained that the assessment at the end of this week will test our physical fitness and willingness to follow instructions. The initiation ceremony will be a test of our strength and bravery, only if we pass both events will we be accepted into the clan and be permitted to wear the clan tattoos.

One of the cubs asked what was going to be involved in the initiation ceremony. Owen appeared to think for a moment before confirming that he's prepared to show us a part of the ceremony but not all otherwise it will not be a true test, would we like to see the part he's offering to show us? Naturally we all nodded enthusiastically in agreement.

What followed was yet another surprise for me, in fact it had been a day full of them! Kurt stepped forward as a volunteer and another clan member was chosen to match him in age and build. By now they were the only two in the centre of the circle for we had returned to the circle of clan members. On Owens command they both stripped down to their underwear, throwing their clothes into the crowd and faced each other in a crouching stance. The clan started chanting and clapping their hands as Owen stepped forward to act as referee. On his word they started to wrestle with the aim to be the first to remove the other one's underwear. Kurt managed to pull off the other's shorts but the wrestling continued, even more aggressively in fact, before with a lot of scrapping Kurt lost his briefs. I found it both compelling and erotic watching these two guys, now wrestling totally naked with their skin shiny from sweat. Looking around I wasn't the only one turn on for many of the clan members were also sporting tent poles.

After about twenty minutes both men were tiring and to my dismay Kurt was pinned to floor and Owen declared him to be the loser. Standing victorious over him, Kurt's foe ordered Kurt to give him a blow job, which he did until the victor was rock hard. From the sideline a clan member threw the victor a sachet of lube who caught it and lubed himself up. Clearly experienced in these matters Kurt simply nodded and crouched down on all fours presenting his backside to the victor. For the next five minutes Kurt was vigorously fucked doggy style, all the while Kurt wanked himself off until he cum followed swiftly by the victor. While this was going on the other clan members took their cocks out and jerked off too sending their jism spraying over both guys at the centre of the circle. I was so turned on that I joined in the circle jerk although I did feel very uncomfortable about wanking myself off in public.

With the spectacle over Owen thanked everyone for their participation before calling it a day and announced that the new applicants will be initiated sometime between the end of the stay at Ebensburg and before the next rally at Gettysburg.

I followed Kurt and Logan back to the trailer too stunned to speak, although as I waited for Kurt to emerge from his shower I did take the opportunity to ask Logan how his date with Perry went. Knowing that I was Perry's best friend Logan was a little cagey with me, all he would say that it went okay and that hopefully their paths would cross again real soon. I didn't get a chance to question him further as Kurt walked into the room and laid down on the sofa with his head in my lap, still naked from the shower.

The three of us went over the plans for the next few days and having noted Kurt's relaxed attitude I casually asked

"When will I get the chance to fuck you like got fucked in the ring back there?" and nodded in the direction of the grassy square.

Just as casually Kurt replied "In the clan there is a strict hierarchy, the more senior of the pairing is the dominant and the junior is passive. So you will always be passive to my active unless I allow otherwise."

"Oh, okay" I replied a little disappointed for Kurt did have a gorgeous arse "just as well I love you fucking me then."

"The pleasure's all mine young man" he replied with a wink "now I think it's time to continue with your training. So, quick as you like strip your clothes off. Don't mind Logan here, I will need his help shortly."

Not waiting for an answer Kurt headed off to our bedroom leaving me to obediently strip naked while Logan enjoyed the view and didn't hide the fact. Kurt returned within a minute carrying the large holdall bag containing the toys that he had bought at the tattoo parlour. After rummaging around he triumphantly brandished his prize, the enema kit. Using the kitchen tap he filled the large enema bag with tepid water and then attached the rubber tubing. Rejoining us he instructed me to kneel down on the floor with my bum in the air and using my hands spread my cheeks. He then asked Logan to open a can of Crisco and grease my anus.

More than happy to oblige Logan did as he was asked and before I knew it I felt some of the grease being smeared round my hole. Then his slim fingers pushed more grease inside and spread it all around before withdrawing to be replaced by the rubber tubing. Kurt stood over me holding the enema bag up high while Logan slowly inserted the tubing further up my rectum. I remained in this position for several minutes until Kurt announced that the bag was empty, squatting down beside me he palpated my stomach before allowing me to dash to the bathroom to evacuate the water and faeces mixture. We repeated the cleaning out process several times with the tubing travelling deeper into me each time until the water ran out clear and clean.

On returning from my final visit to the toilet I found both Kurt and Logan stark naked with Kurt busy greasing up his erect cock. Pushed to the floor and on all fours I was first fucked by Kurt, who like the other night shoved his cock up me in one brutal thrust. This time I knew better than to protest, actually I never got the chance to for as my mouth opened in response to the anal onslaught Logan's cock slipped inside. Willingly I sucked on his flaccid cock which rapidly sprang to life with my tongue action. Kurt's fucking was rough and vocal, egged on by Logan who by now was fucking my mouth. I heard Kurt warn him not to cum in my mouth as there was a better place to deposit it so Logan eased off leaving enough action to keep me occupied and him aroused. Kurt on the other hand seemed intent on cramming as much of his cock into me as hard as he could and unsurprisingly he came with a final thrust sending his jism shooting up my rectum. He unceremoniously pulled out while Logan slipped out of my mouth and straight up my arse. Not being unkind to Logan Kurt was much thicker so accommodating Logan was easier, the only thing I didn't realise was that Logan was longer than Kurt. So as he slid in up to the hilt I felt him hit my inner ring making me wince and I flushed a bright red.

"Sorry" I heard him say.

"It's okay. I've just never had anything go in that deep. Give me a minute to relax and you'll be through" I replied keeping my fingers crossed.

I took deep breaths and willed myself to relax, sure enough, slowly but surely my resistance diminished until with a sigh from behind me I felt the head of his cock push past my ring and up into my bowels. It was a peculiar feeling having both rings with a shaft sliding past them at the same time, but I liked it. So much so that by the time Kurt had returned to the room having rinsed his cock off in the bathroom I was grinding back on Logan with all my might.

When Logan finally shot his load up me, Kurt took his place immediately not even giving me time to adjust my position. This cycle was repeated until from my estimate they had both been up me at least three times and from their comments my hole was now very sloppy and full of jism. Logan complained that he was unable to get any friction now, Kurt grinned saying that he had an idea. So with Kurt sprawled out on the sofa I climbed on top and rode his cock like I was riding a horse. I bounced up and down enjoying the new position and kissing Kurt whenever I could, then I felt movement behind me and a hand placed itself on my back. The hand pushed me down towards Kurt who wrapped his hands tight around my chest preventing me from moving, within a couple of seconds I felt something press between my anal ring and Kurt's impaling cock. It was of course Logan's cockhead and after some wriggling around from me and persistent pushing from Logan he slowly and carefully slid alongside Kurt's cock.

This was a first for me, I'd never been double fucked before and again initially it was a peculiar feeling. I felt incredibly full until I got accustomed to the double intrusion and then they started moving around inside me as if vying for best position. Actually what they were doing was slowly fucking me but at a slightly different pace so they might be at some points moving in the same direction and at other times in opposite directions. Very strange, but very addictive and very good for stretching my ring even wider, so Kurt informed me at one point. Unfortunately this couldn't last and so after the two guys had cum once again they informed me that they were spent.

I thought that was it for me and I would be allowed to go to bed, but no, I was cleaned out again to remove all that jism and any new faeces. As I wiped myself dry on some paper towelling Kurt retrieved from the holdall a medium sized butt plug and having lightly greased it up made me sit down on it. Given all the action my anus had seen this evening it was quite easy for me to sink down on it and swallow the exaggerated head in one go. My ring was so tired it was only able to lightly grip onto the neck of the plug. Kurt must have realised that I might have difficulty keeping the plug in because he handed me my boxer shorts and told me to keep it in place until I was told to take it out again.

It was only after we had cleared the lounge up and had our showers that I was allowed to take the butt plug out. It was a relief if I'm honest because my hole was so sore and tired from the stretching and pounding it had received. I mentioned this fact to Kurt who just laughed and told me that this was just the beginning. In bed, spooned together in our usual fashion I asked Kurt if he really loved me or was I just a pawn in a game he was playing.

Holding me tight against his chest he said "I swear I love you more than anything or anyone else in the world. Please don't ever doubt that. I have never been happier and I feel complete now that you are my cub. Do you believe me?"

I nodded satisfied and snuggled even further into his enfolding arms.

The following morning once again Kurt was up before me and nowhere to be found. I wandered into the lounge where I found a note from Kurt telling me to get washed and shaved, then clean myself out and reinsert the butt plug I wore last night. Oh and then I had to wear the clothes he had laid out for me – jock strap, jeans, T-shirt and walking boots. Sighing I did as I was told, well except that I had breakfast first then went for my shower etc. I quite enjoyed giving myself an enema it was quite erotic in fact, the feeling of the rubber tube sliding deep inside me with the water gently flowing into me. So was the feel of the greased butt plug as my anal ring expanded over the rapidly flaring head of the plug, this time I had to relax a little for my ring had tightened up slightly overnight. But soon enough I had it fully inserted, gripping the neck tightly as I got dressed in the clothes as instructed.

I spent the day helping the rally crew set the trade stands up and the other clan members wherever and whenever I was needed. All throughout the morning that plug stayed buried inside my rectum, by mid-morning I had almost forgotten it was there. Then at lunchtime I joined Kurt, Logan and Dexter where they were still kitting out a trade stand. Together we sat on the grass and ate sandwiches downed with a can of beer each. We were clearing up and I was ready to return to where I had been working when Kurt abruptly told me to stand up, drop my jeans and bend over. I hesitated looking around at the other crew and clan members in the vicinity but none are taking any notice of me. So I stood up and undid my jeans before pushing them down, then I bent over facing away from Kurt and grasped my knees for stability. I felt Kurt step up behind me, take hold of the butt plug and gently pull it out before reinserting it, drawing a groan from me. There was a short and quiet discussion between Dexter and Kurt while at the same time Kurt slowly fucked me with the butt plug. With a final push Kurt left the plug buried inside me and then told me to pull my jeans up again. As I did so I heard Dexter tell Kurt that in his opinion I was ready for the next size up.

That evening was pretty much a re-run of the previous evening, once back in the trailer that is. After the evening meal I was told to strip and then sent to the bathroom to thoroughly clean myself out again. For the next hour I was relentlessly fucked by Kurt and Logan in turn before twice being double fucked, after which they were spent for the time being. I was so into this scene that I just loved my status as a cum-dump for Kurt and Logan and if I'm honest I could have happily carried on like this for hours. I took a five minute break on the toilet to let out the load of jism deposited earlier, on my return to the lounge my eyes nearly popped out of their sockets.

Kurt had removed from the holdall bag a huge dildo. It was double ended and about ten inches long, very thick, possibly as thick as a coke can. I gulped audibly but Kurt merely smiled encouragingly telling me that I would be able to swallow it whole if I took my time and relaxed. I stood there and watched him liberally grease it up with Crisco, then holding it in a vertical position he told me to sit down on it. Still uncertain I knelt down where indicated and let him guide me until my anus was positioned directly over the dildo. I sank down until it was just pressing against my ring, then with deep breaths I used my weight to impale myself on the monster dildo. I slowly slid down further and further until I thought I could not get any more inside me, already it had breached my inner ring! I asked Kurt how more was there, to which he replied about another inch. So with sheer determination I sat down with my cheeks pressed against the floor driving the dildo fully inside. My ring closed gratefully behind it and I cried out with the overwhelming fullness that was inside me. Sweat poured from my face as I wondered how long I could keep it inside.

I went to get up when I felt Kurt's hands on my shoulders preventing me from moving, he told me to remain motionless and grow accustomed to its size. I my ring spasmed involuntarily and without warning I came sending jets of jism shooting across the room which hit the floor with audible splats. Once I had finished orgasming Kurt allowed me to relax my anus, resulting in the dildo sliding out of me with a squelchy fart and bouncing across the floor, leaving a slimy trail behind it. Thank goodness it was a wooden floor! I was so embarrassed I stammered an apology but Logan held his hand up to silence me.

"Hey man, no harm has been done" he assured me.

Kurt however was more stern with me "You should have caught the dildo with your hand as it slid out but never mind. On this occasion I will overlook the matter. Go and give yourself another clean out while I clear this mess up."

Still feeling embarrassed I could think of nothing to say in response so I simply did as I was told and gave my greasy sloppy hole another douching. More air came out loudly like cannon shots which only added to my embarrassment because I heard chuckling coming from the lounge. When I returned to the lounge Kurt was busy greasing up a large butt plug, with a grin on his face he told me to turn around and bend over spreading my legs at the same time.

I didn't have the energy to argue so I simply followed his instructions and waited for the inevitable. Despite its large size I had little difficulty in accepting the intrusion, even when it got to the widest part. My anal ring was just too exhausted to offer resistance in fact it could barely grip on to the neck of the plug at all. Like the night before I had to keep the plug in so without guidance I grabbed my shorts and put them on before the plug had a chance to slip out again.

By the time we got ready for bed it was getting late but Kurt showed no signs of being tired, he seemed to have caught his second wind because as I removed the butt plug and washed it thoroughly in the sink he told me to leave my bum all greasy. Evidently he had plans for it, for when I climbed into bed and curled up ready to drift off to sleep he grabbed my legs and rolled me onto my stomach. Although shattered I obediently opened my legs but my eyes were a different matter, they kept closing of their own accord. All too soon I felt Kurt slipping his cock up me and he was right in what he said the other night. After the intense anal and rectal stretching I had endured in the last twenty four hours taking his cock was a piece of cake and I'm ashamed to say he slid inside me with no resistance at all.

"That's better" Kurt whispered in my ear as he lay on top of me with his cock fully buried in my backside. "I love holes where I can just slide inside."

"Mmmm that feels good" I murmured drowsily as he began to gently fuck me.

It didn't take him long to shoot another load up me but he seemed in no hurry to leave as he lay there kissing my neck and shoulders until he was flaccid once more and slipped out of me naturally. I felt him climb off me backwards but remained somewhere between my outstretched legs. The next thing I felt were his fingers playing with my hole, teasing and stroking it before sliding in up the knuckle by the feel of it. The first couple I barely registered, in fact the third was easy and so was the fourth but I could at least feel them by now. They withdrew before returning arranged slightly differently in what felt like a cone shape, a bit like a butt plug I guess. Now he had my attention so opening my eyes I lifted my head and adjusted my position so that I could look over my shoulder. Just in time to see his coned hand sliding in up to the widest part of his hand, the last set of knuckles.

Unconsciously I clamped shut without meaning to and received a stinging slap on my bum from Kurt who frowned showing his displeasure.

"Relax goddamit I was nearly there" he growled at me and raised his hand ready to slap my bum again.

"Sorry Kurt I didn't mean to but this is a first for me you know" I replied with just a hint of tiredness induced irritation in my voice.

"Well it might be your first, but it sure hell aint going to be the last time you get my fist up your cute little backside I can assure you. Your hole was made for being fisted. Now relax like a good boy and let me in" he said in his authoritive voice.

"Mmmm" was all I replied as I took deep breaths and concentrated on relaxing my ring for him.

A few moments later I felt his hand slide smoothly past my ring and ball up into a fist, I sighed in relief as much as in pleasure knowing that I had satisfied my man. What followed was a gentle fisting which eventually brought me to my second orgasm of the evening, by then I was laying on my back with Kurt's fist buried inside my rectum and my cock being sucked lovingly by him. I drifted off to sleep with his fist still inside me.

Chapter 8 – Stretching to new limits

The following day was identical to the previous one except this time the place was crowded with the public attending the rally. So although I kept the large butt plug in place all day I did not get inspected by Kurt or other clan members, we were simply too busy and there was no privacy anywhere. By the time evening came my hole had been stretched so much that the butt plug practically fell out as soon as my jeans were removed.

After the evening meal and we'd washed up both Kurt and Logan fucked me a couple of times but only to serve as a cum dump for them. Then the evening took a slightly different turn, Logan reminded Kurt that there was a soccer match on that they had been planning to watch it. Kurt agreed that it was important to watch the game so while Logan fetched the beers from the fridge Kurt pulled the two sofas together with a gap between them. In the gap he put the coffee table and covered it with several cushions and then a blanket. I stood to one side bemused and watched his antics wondering what he was planning. Then when he was satisfied that everything was in place and that both he and Logan could watch the TV from their seats he called me over.

"I want you to lay on the blanket here, face down and make yourself comfortable" he instructed before heading off into our bedroom.

I did as I was told, still unsure of what was to follow. I was only when Logan returned carrying the beers and sat on the sofa in the seat next to me did I begin to get an inkling on what was going on. My suspicions were confirmed when Kurt returned holding an open can of Crisco sat on the other sofa again in the seat next to me. Grinning to each other they high fived before Logan turned the TV on and used the remote control to find the right channel.

While he did this Kurt set about greasing up my anus and packing loads of Crisco into my rectum. He left it a few minutes as they watched the opening kickoff before returning his attention to my bum. With the grace of an expert he slipped his fist inside my rectum and left it there motionless to allow me to adjust to the intrusion before slowly and gently fisting me. It helped me to have the game to focus on and forget what it would look like if someone happened to walk into the trailer right now! After the first ten minutes or so I lost track of Kurt's fist being smoothly pulled out of my arse completely and then reinserted just as smoothly, perhaps because he was doing it in such a consistent rhythm. At some point during the first half of the soccer match I noticed Kurt get up to go to the toilet, it came as a surprise for I was still being fisted.

I looked over at Logan who grinned at me and said "I've been doing this for the last five minutes and you didn't notice the switch over, did you?"

"I guess not!" I replied matching his grin.

"Are you enjoying the attention your hole is getting?"

"Uh huh, I didn't know it was possible to do what you're doing to me but it sure feels good" I groaned as Logan tickled my inner ring with his fingers.

"That's what I like to hear, but we've really only just begun the stretching process, you'll be amazed by what we're gonna get up there......" he trailed off as Kurt resumed his seat and greased up his hand.

"Don't mind me" Kurt said "you go for it Logan, we need to get past that second ring tonight in any case."

"Sure thing boss" was all Logan said as he started to massage my inner ring in earnest.

It was just after the second half of the soccer game had started that I groaned and bucked a little as Logan's fist finally overcame the inner ring's resistance and his fist slid past it and up into my bowels. As Kurt had done at the beginning of this session Logan kept his arm still while I grew accustomed to the impalement before he pushed further up into me. Five minutes later I felt a tap on my shoulder and as I looked around in response to it I saw that Logan's arm was buried up my arse as far as his elbow.

"Wow! That's incredible" I laughed "You guys are something else."

The rest of the game was spent with Kurt's forearm slowly pistoning in and out of me, by the end of the game both rings had grown so accustomed to being stretched wide that I experienced no discomfort at all. Okay if I'm honest I barely registered the arms presence because I was so loose!

As the games credit's rolled and the presenter did a post match analysis Logan on Kurt's request fetched the largest dildo from the holdall bag and greased it up having placed it on the floor. It was the size of a small fire extinguisher with a flared base to prevent accidental swallowing. Even with all the fisting I had had that evening the dildo was still wider than either of the men's fists so as I sat down on the head of the dildo I felt myself being stretched further. I spent the rest of the evening sitting in a lotus position on the floor with my anus slowly getting stretched ever wider because of the flared base.

When I was eventually allowed to get off the enormous dildo my poor old hole simply could not close up again immediately, in fact it took the whole night to recover. Thankfully Kurt let me rest my hole that night and the following day. By morning it felt a little puffy but had closed up tight again with no apparent damage being done. The only side effect that I did notice was that after going to the toilet my stools seemed to be twice the width that they had previously been.

In hindsight it was just as well that I was being rested for today was even busier than yesterday had been, principally because it was the last day of the rally for the public to attend. Wanting to earn as many dollars as possible the rally crew and clan kept the event running for an extra hour due to the hot weather and large number of attendees. This was great for business but bad news for us as we didn't get back to the trailer until late in the evening.

I thought that in view of this I might have a respite from the training but I was wrong for I was told in no uncertain terms that my hole would be getting a workout regardless of the time of night. The day of assessment and initiation was fast approaching and I needed to be ready for it. So while Kurt and Logan prepared the evening meal I cleaned myself out and inserted the large butt plug before getting dressed again ready for the meal. Afterwards I was told to strip naked in front of them and bend over at the waist, which I did without hesitation. Kurt then took hold of the butt plug and firmly pulled it out with a loud plop. He and Logan stood next to each other and for a couple of minutes they discussed the state of my ring and how much work they had left to do tonight.

Then without further ado Kurt greased up his hand and slipped it in me as easy as anything, within a couple of heartbeats he had pushed all the way in up to his elbow. Despite myself I groaned in reaction and braced myself against the thrust. He slowly increased his speed until he was truly fist fucking my hole, not quite pulling out before pistoning back in again. Logan stepped in front of me and I took him in my mouth sucking him to erection. I focussed on giving him a great blow job not stopping until I had swallowed all his jism and sucked him back to being flaccid.

Only then did he step away and swap positions with Kurt and we started all over again. Having swallowed two loads of jism I was told to kneel on the sofa facing away from them with legs spread. The fisting continued, this time they alternated with first Kurt inserting his fist then as he withdrew Logan inserted his. They continued like this for several minutes slowly getting faster and closer together until they overlapped with one fist still being in me while the other was trying to enter too.

Finally the overlapping was complete and I realised with a jolt that I was being double fisted! I could feel their hands moving around inside me, clasped together they formed a giant fist. They pushed up inside me passing through the inner ring after several attempts until they were stopped at the elbow as I was unable to stretch any further.

I felt a familiar pressure building up inside, having warned my two assailants we shuffled backwards until I was standing on the floor again bent over at the waist. As the pistoning started once more the sensations I experienced became too much and I spontaneously shot my load all over the floor without once touching myself. I was so grateful when Kurt declared himself satisfied with my progress that in his opinion my training was now over and I could now rest for the evening.

My poor old hole was so loose and sloppy that as I washed myself off in the shower I feared that it might never close up again. It would of course, as time would tell, that along with the helpful pelvic floor exercises that Kurt had shown me how to do.

The next morning it was all systems go as we helped pack up the site before setting off in the direction of Gettysburg in one large convoy. After a while the conversation between Kurt and me naturally dried up as it tends to do when the driver (Kurt this time) needs to concentrate on driving. I was still tired from the night before and drifted off into a light sleep only to be woken with a jolt a little later as we left the highway and drove up a bumpy farm track.

For a quarter of a mile we drove along this track until came across a clearly abandoned and derelict farm, you would never have found it unless you already had prior knowledge so I wondered what we were doing here at all. We were soon to find out. Once all of the trailers were parked up Owen called a clan meeting and we stood there in the old farmyard in front of him expectantly waiting to hear why we had stopped at this place.

"Folks" Owen said in a confident manner "we have set up camp here on the recommendation of a couple of our fellow biker clans who have used this site before. They have assured me that we will not be disturbed as it is not listed on any map so no one will drop by out of curiosity. Now I expect you will be wondering why we have stopped, the answer is simple, we have four cubs due to be assessed and initiated into the clan and this is the perfect place to do it."

There was a gentle round of applause and a couple of whistles from the crowd before Owen continued his speech.

"Would the four cubs now step forward and remove their clothes until they are naked so the assessment can commence."

I along with the three other guys stepped out of the crowd until we were halfway between them and Owen, then standing in a row we undressed. As each item of clothing was removed we threw them into a pile in front of Owen until we were standing stark naked. I noticed that like me none of them tried to cover their nudity and also that their bodies had been waxed too, somehow that made me feel a whole lot better about my hairlessness. We smiled a little nervously at one another before turning to face Owen again. Owen requested that our clothes be taken away for safekeeping and a clan member immediately ran over, scooped them up before he carried them to the nearest trailer.

He was about to start talking to us when all of a sudden there was a great roaring of motorcycle engines, startled, we looked in the direction of the noise to see over a hundred motorcycles coming up the farm track! I gulped now feeling very vulnerable being naked but Owen appeared totally cool with this development and actually welcomed them in. As the engines were silenced and the bikers walked into the yard Owen informed them that they were just in time to witness the cubs' assessment and initiation ceremony. This was met with more whoops and cheers from the mean looking leather clad men as they crowded into the farm yard straining to get a good view of us cubs.

I tried to ignore the sniggers and lewd remarks from the audience as Owen inspected every inch of our bodies to ensure that we were totally hair-free. At last satisfied that we were he instructed us to do press ups and other fitness exercises to demonstrate our strength and suppleness. While we were doing the exercises I noticed movement off to one side, it was Dexter and Logan messing around with a hose pipe seeking a working tap to get water from. Giving up, well the farm was abandoned after all, they resorted to connecting the hosepipe to one of the trailers.

Clearly happy with their lateral thinking they unravelled the hosepipe reel until the end of the hosepipe lay at Owen's feet. Its purpose became apparent when Dexter disappeared and then returned holding an open can of Crisco which he offered to Owen. He however shook his head and nodded in our direction. His meaning was clear we were to grease ourselves up ready for whatever happened next. Dexter offered the can to the first cub who smiled a little tentatively before scooping out a little of the grease and smeared along his crack and around his anus. This was repeated with the other two cubs and finally me. As I greased up my hole I looked up to see Kurt standing in front of me, he smiled encouragingly and gave me a bug thumbs up. I mirrored his actions to show that I was okay with what was going on.

Dexter handed Owen the can of Crisco while he asked one of the clan members to turn on the water in the trailer that fed the hosepipe. Between the two of them they managed with some comical negotiating to get the water flowing at the right speed and at the right temperature. Owen told us to assume the douching position i.e. on all fours with our bums raised in the air. Then one by one Dexter inserted the hosepipe into each of us, letting the water flow inside until our stomachs were distended, only then would he move onto the next cub. The water filled cubs had to remain in position until all four of us had been done. Then having cleared access to the nearest drain we were allowed to dash over to it and evacuate the filthy effluent down it. This process was repeated another three times until everyone could see the effluent running clean as we squatted over the drain.

Standing once more in a line in front of Owen we were told to turn round, bend over and present our bums for inspection by spreading our own cheeks. It wasn't the most dignified of positions standing bent over at the waist with my arms reaching backwards and my hands pulling my cheeks apart. But it was erotic at the same time, knowing that my anus was on view for all to see while the warm afternoon breeze blew over it making it quiver.

Owen then called over our bears, in my case Kurt, and in front of us they greased up their hands from the can of Crisco Owen was holding out to them. As they walked round behind us we were told to relax and allow our bears in, no guessing where. I felt Kurt's fingers play briefly with my hole before coning them and smoothly push easily into me. He stopped with just his fist resting in my rectum for this was just a demonstration that I had been anally trained to the required level. Looking over my shoulder I saw that the other three cubs were in the same position as me and by their expressions had taken their bear's fists with equal ease. I heard from behind me Owen announce that we had passed the assessment and that the initiation ceremony could begin.

As I stood up Kurt slipped out of me and patted me on the bum with his greasy hand. Before he was lost in the crowd he kissed me on the top of my head and congratulated me on passing the assessment, just the initiation to go! We moved en masse out of the farm yard and into an overgrown meadow.

The bikers and clan members reformed into a ring with us cubs in the centre; it was time for the wrestling matches to begin. As with the wrestling match that Kurt had demonstrated when we arrived at Ebensburg, the loser in our wrestling matches would be pinned to the ground and fucked by the winner as punishment. We wrestled each other in turn, spurred on by the cheering of our audience and the knowledge of the penalty for losing. Each match was intensely erotic to the extent that I and the other three cubs sported erections throughout the matches. We weren't the only ones to find watching two naked men straining and grappling with each other a turn on judging by the bulges in many of the men's trousers.

I lost only one match, the last one as it happened because by then I was at the point of exhaustion and having looked into the handsome face of my opponent I decided losing wouldn't be so bad after all. He fucked me in the missionary position pinning my feet either side of my shoulders which gave him total access to my hole. Sorry Kurt but I really enjoyed that fuck, both of us were worn out and barely had the energy for the fuck so he took it nice and slow allowing me to enjoy every stroke of his cock inside me. Not only that I had time to look around and up into the many faces of our audience, each one displayed a mixture of enjoyment of the entertainment and outright lust. Just when I thought he wasn't able to cum inside me, he did, with a groan and a shudder he collapsed on top of me to a round of applause from the bikers.

Disentangling ourselves we stood up and joined the other two cubs while we waited for the winner to be announced. We didn't have long to wait for there were only four of us, unfortunately I came second but I was pleased with the result and from Kurt's cheering so was he. Owen shook each of our hands and thanked us for putting on such an entertaining performance, he then declared that the second part of the initiation was about to begin.

The crowd of bikers parted like a wave before us as four of their comrades wheeled in their motorbikes to the centre of the ring. Each of us cubs were dragged over to them and bent over the back of the bikes so that our stomachs were resting on the seats and our bums hanging off the end of the bike. We were permitted to place our legs either side to help support ourselves. Out wrists were then handcuffed to the bike effectively holding us in position. The bikes had been laid out in a cross formation enabling us to watch what was happening to our neighbours on either side. As Owen explained to the audience that they were entitled to either fuck or fist a cub, but only one cub and only one action per person was permitted for the cub's sake. Dexter went round to each of us and re-greased our holes and packed loads of Crisco up into our rectums in preparation.

What followed was a two hour fuck and fistathon with our holes being constantly filled with cocks initially until we were gaping so slack and open that the bikers could no longer get a satisfying fuck. So they moved onto fisting us at first gently and considerately while they wanked themselves off sending load after load of jism over our backs and legs. However by the end of the session even a fist wasn't touching the sides so they moved onto either plunging their fists in up to the elbow to get some feeling from our inner rings or double fisted us. Personally I was so mentally spaced out I barely registered much after the first dozens fistings, it was all the same me. All I knew was that I had a biker in me and I loved it. Okay by the end of the initiation I was getting a little sore but not once did I want them to stop cramming their fists and/or arms up me.

All good things must come to an end and as the final biker spewed his jism over the cub next to me Owen clapped his hands pronouncing the end of the initiation ceremony. First we were released from our handcuffs and as we stood up we stretched our stiff bodies from being in one position for so long. Next, still a little wobbly on our feet we were escorted back to the farm yard and hosed down to remove the caked on layers of dried jism. Lastly we were hosed out on the inside too flushing out what felt like pints of jism and Crisco mixture. While all this was going on our bears had retrieved our clothing, with the other clan members and bikers lined up in neat rows as if it was a military parade ground.

In a way I guess it was for after a long amusing speech by Owen and Dexter the four of us were told that we had each passed the initiation ceremony. From now on we would be classed as full members of the clan with all the benefits and responsibilities that came with it. Finally we were handed back our clothes and allowed to get dressed, which for me was a relief for the sun was setting and the air was rapidly cooling plus I was feeling a little sunburnt from all the exposure to the sun this afternoon. As we dressed Dexter confirmed that we could now re-grow our body hair and arrange for our tattoos to be done.

I woke up totally disorientated to find I was in a bed, naked and in total darkness. Where was I? Who was I? Why am I naked? Slowly it all came back to me. I remembered Kurt guiding, well more like carrying me, back to our trailer and into the bedroom. I was so exhausted I put up no resistance when he pulled back the duvet cover and undressed me before telling me to get some rest. I fell asleep so quickly that I never even heard him shut the bedroom door behind him.

I laid there all snug and warm just listening to the muffled sounds of the TV and Kurt's voice as he talked to Logan. Curiosity and hunger got the better of me, so I climbed out of bed and pulled on a pair of boxers before wandering all bleary eyed into the lounge. Rubbing my eyes to get the last of the sleep out of them I asked Kurt the time, only to be shocked when he informed me that it was 11:30pm. I'd slept nearly six hours solid, no wonder I was starving!

Kurt must have read my mind for he made a bee line for the kitchen and made me a large plate of toast and butter which I consumed within minutes to the amusement of the other two. Once my hunger was satiated I sat back and made small talk before asking the inevitable question of how did I do this afternoon? Obviously I passed but I just wanted reassurance, which I got in heaps from both Kurt and Logan.

I nearly fell out of my seat when Kurt told me that he was so proud of the way I have handled the whole training and initiation process that he thought I ought to be rewarded by being allowed to fuck him. My mouth dropped open in shock, all I could do was nod indicating that I would like to do so and asked when? Right now was the answer, so in record time Kurt went to clean himself out while I made my way into the bedroom.

I didn't have long to wait for Kurt seemed as keen as I was to enjoy this role reversal, as he entered the bedroom he opened the can of Crisco and taking a small glob of it greased up his hole and then my raging hard on. Still very much the alpha male he took charge and lay on his back pulling his legs up close to his chest, nicely exposing his hole to me. Concentrating I aimed my cock head towards his hole and gently pushed my way in. I needn't have worried for he was clearly no virgin and in no time at all I was inside him buried up to the hilt and thrusting away like there was no tomorrow. When I was close to cumming Kurt asked me to stop and called out to Logan to join us for some fun.

"I thought you were never going to ask!" he laughed as he entered our bedroom already standing to attention.

I heard the can of Crisco being moved and guessed that Logan was using the grease to lube himself up, which was exactly what he had done. Next I felt the bed shift under his weight as he climbed on to join us, I didn't have long to find out what his intentions were for within a couple of seconds his cock was pressing against my anus. I didn't try to put up any resistance, I'm not sure I could if I had, as I liked Logan and having sex with him was good too.

So before I knew it I was being fucked by Logan while fucking Kurt, heaven in a word! Logan and I must have cum a good couple of times before we disengaged pulling our jism covered cocks out of the respective holes. I went to clean myself up when Kurt asked me where I was going for the fun had just begun. Rejoining them on the bed Kurt got up onto all fours and told me to pack his arse with grease because he wanted a fist up him, it's been a while since he had this pleasure.

I did as I was told with a big happy grin on my face, this day just got better and better! A few minutes later I found myself kneeling behind him pushing my coned hand slowly into his willing backside. As my hand slid smoothly out of sight and further into his rectum I felt Logan playing with my hole. I looked over at him and with a grin I too got down on all fours to allow him easier access to my stretched out hole. Needless to say he was inside within seconds as my hole was still very soft and sloppy from this afternoon. I was really getting into the swing of this when out of the corner of my eye I noticed Kurt indicating to Logan to pass over the Crisco and move a little closer.

Logan nodded his acceptance and momentarily pulled out of me as he fetched the can of grease and gave it to Kurt before reinserting his fist up me and presenting his bum for inspection. Five minutes later we had formed a fisting circle with much squelching going on as our fists plunged deep into holes and then were pulled out totally leaving a gaping cavern behind. This went on for a little while before an idea formed in my head, one that seemed fitting for the occasion. So I called a halt to the proceedings and told Kurt and Logan what I wanted them to do, a little surprised by my assertiveness they did as instructed.

Having disengaged I climbed off the bed, fetched the can of Crisco and walked round to the bottom of the bed and knelt down facing it. Meanwhile they had crawled to where I was kneeling and got onto their backs pulling their knees back against their chests. As soon as they were comfortable and in the right position for me I packed a load more Crisco into their rectums, which was followed by my fists slipping right on in with ease. For the next half an hour I fist fucked the two guys in sync, thrusting in and out of their holes getting ever deeper and faster. By the time they could hold back no longer and needed to wank themselves off to orgasm I was plunging my fists into them right up to my elbow and almost beyond but not quite. Once their orgasms had subsided I gently withdrew and fetched masses of kitchen roll to clean us up with, needless to say the shower was working overtime for the next half an hour washing our grease off inside and out.

Afterwards we sat around the dining table drinking a well earned cup of coffee making small talk and discussing our session in the bedroom just now. That is until Kurt saw the time on the kitchen clock, it was nearly 1:00am and we had to be up early in the morning. We still had to drive to Gettysburg and set up the rally. A few minutes later, having quickly tidied up, I laid in bed curled up in Kurt's arms feeling content knowing that I was now officially part of the clan and that from now on my name was Danny Honaw. The only question now was, what do I do about my job back home?

A BIKER'S TALE – PART 2 (RUNNING WITH THE PACK)

Chapter 1 – The return to Colonie

The alarm clock rang loudly in my ears jolting me awake with a groan. My hands clawed blindly at the bedside cabinet desperately seeking the source of that torturous noise. Triumph at last! A finger had found the snooze button bringing immediate silence to the room. Leisurely I stretched my body out beneath the duvet and with a foot I stroked the leg of my still sleeping lover, Kurt. He simply grumbled under his breath and pulled the duvet higher over his head.

I sighed to myself knowing that we couldn't afford to idly lie around, for there was work to be done and Gettysburg to be reached this morning. If not, we would be working late into the night to set the rally up in preparation for tomorrow. I rolled out of bed and stood up gingerly feeling my bum which, not surprisingly, was aching from all the attention it had received yesterday. I dressed quickly and headed for the kitchen to start cooking our breakfast. The smell of frying bacon did the job, within ten minutes I was joined by both Kurt and Logan who sat around the kitchen table waiting impatiently for their food.

As we ploughed through the bacon sandwiches there was a knock on the trailer door and in walked Owen not waiting for a reply. He greeted us in his customary cheerful manner and once again congratulated me on joining the clan with such enthusiasm. This naturally led onto his real purpose for the visit which was to ask me (okay, tell me but in a nice way) to drive back up to Colonie taking Marvin, Zac and Nathan (the other three cubs) with me. He had arranged with Levi for us to stay over with him while he does our tattoos. Crikey I thought to myself, he doesn't hang around! But as I glanced around the room I appeared to be the only one surprised by this development, so I smiled and nodded my agreement with his 'request' before preparing myself for the coming journey.

An hour later we were speeding along the Interstate 78 in my little old car loaded down with three passengers and a boot full of our belongings. Initially there was silence in the car as I concentrated on the road and traffic around me while the others appeared lost in their own thoughts as they gazed out at the passing scenery. For my part I reflected on my recent parting from Kurt. As I had packed my travel bag in preparation for the impending journey Kurt had grabbed me by the waist and spun me round in his arms before giving me a rib-cracking bear hug. Releasing me momentarily I gasped for air only for it to be sucked back out of my lungs as he kissed me passionately on the lips and enveloped me in his arms once more. I could not help but become aroused and desperately wanted to push Kurt onto the bed for a quick fuck but there was no time and I had to make do with a fondle of Kurt's packet straining behind his jeans. Laughing he slapped me on my behind and promised to see to my needs on my return. With that he stepped back, told me to drive carefully and then disappeared to start preparing the trailer for its own journey.

All this reminiscing had stirred my loins and I tried to discreetly adjust my position but could not stop myself from smiling at the thought of keeping Kurt to his promise. I just didn't know how I was going to cope with being celibate for a whole week! Zac, who was sitting in the front passenger seat glanced over at me and broke the silence by asking me what I had been thinking about.

I returned his glance and for the first time I noticed how attractive Zac was. His skin was like milk chocolate complimented by his dark brown eyes and black hair in ringlets which sat on top of his head like an unruly mop. This combined with his easy smile and animated manner created a "wild child" impression. I had seen very little of him around the camp and the only time we had really interacted had been at the initiation ceremony, which hadn't been to make small talk. I blushed red from the memory of how much I had enjoyed fucking Zac doggy style in front of all the bikers and clan members after winning our wrestling match.

"Uh...." I started off trying to think of the right words to say "oh, I was just thinking about Kurt and then I remembered about our wrestling match........" I trailed off feeling my cheeks go even redder from embarrassment.

Zac burst out laughing and replied "Heck that was one hell of a day! Great fun but my arse sure ached afterwards. My hole was so stretched I thought it would never close up again!"

Two voices piped up from the back seats as their owners, Marvin and Nathan, leant forward and joined in with the conversation. The topic of which turned to our respective partners and it quickly became apparent to me that all four of us were what you'd call the "bottoms" in our relationships. Not that any of us were complaining as we freely admitted to each other. There's nothing better than having something inserted up your rectum and preferably bigger the better! The only thing which I kept to myself was the fact that I appeared to be the only one who had ever "topped" his bear.

This conversation went backwards and forwards for what seemed like forever but at least it served to pass the time as we continued on with the monotonous journey along the motorway. We made only the occasional convenience break to stretch our limbs and empty our bladders before heading off again. About halfway through our journey we stopped at a roadside diner and enjoyed a huge burger meal washed down with loads of cola and chips on the side, just in case we didn't eat again until much later. Well that was the excuse we told ourselves. Finally we arrived in Colonie and pulled up at Levi's tattoo parlour just as the sun was setting, I had been driving nearly all day and I was exhausted!

I knocked loudly on the front door for it wasn't obvious if anybody was actually, the place was in darkness from what we could see. I was just about to know again when Levi opened the door and greeted us with a big grin on his face.

"Fetch your bags and come on in lads, I've been looking forward to having you stay with me ever since I heard the news that you'd passed your tests" he said enthusiastically.

We did as requested and as the last one, Marvin, carried his travel bag in through the front door Levi locked it securely behind him. Levi led us through to the back of the shop and into his lounge which I recognised from the last visit I had made with Kurt. Not stopping he bid us follow him up the stairs onto the landing and past the "massage parlour" where I had suffered the extremely painful body waxing. At the end of the corridor we entered a large room which ran the width of the building but only had one window facing the rear of the property. Initially it appeared to be empty with bare wooden floorboards, except for curtains and a large chest of drawers next to the window.

However behind us, stood leant against the wall were four single mattresses and a pile of sheets, blankets and pillows. Seeing our surprised expressions Levi chuckled and explained that he hadn't set the beds up because he didn't know what our preferred sleeping arrangements would be. We were free to have four single beds; two doubles or one huge bed depending on how the fancy took us he finished with a wink. He then told us to leave our bags in the room; we would have time to unpack later, and led us back down to the living area. As we made ourselves comfortable Levi asked if we liked Pizza, I nodded vigorously as I was by now starving and out of the corner of my eye I could see the others doing the same. That settled the matter, Levi made a quick telephone call and twenty minutes later we were tucking into deep crust pizzas with extra topping!

It didn't take long for us to clear our plates, no sooner had we put our knives and forks down than the lounge door opened and to my surprise a man walked in carrying an empty tray ready to take our dirty plates away. I guess he was probably about twenty years younger than Levi and of Thai or Chinese descent. Either way he was very petit and pretty, if you like the feminine type. He greeted us warmly and Levi introduced him as Sanun, his partner for the last ten years and who shared all of his interests. He would be helping out during our stay. Having cleared the table he brought forth another tray laden with homemade cakes and a large pot of coffee to which we helped ourselves while Levi disappeared upstairs to retrieve the finished artwork on our tattoos.

Once we had had our fill and the table cleared once more Levi spread out the drawings he had done. The work was stunning and both Levi and Sanun were clearly proud of it, I just wish I could be half the artist that he was! Naturally I studied mine first and I verbalised my admiration of the artwork, there had been some changes made which Levi explained had been done for both practical and artistic reasons. Medusa's black bat-like wings had been replaced with white feathered wings (to decrease the amount of heavy inking required) and the sword had gone altogether. She was still holding the decapitated head of Perseus aloft with one hand but now she was supporting her weight with a bloodied hand on the headless body (it made the scene more gruesome because the viewer would know that he had been beheaded by her own hands). From the neck of the corpse blood flowed in rivulets down what would be my spine and disappearing between my bum cheeks. A hand still reached out towards the viewer and the shield still bore the message "History is littered with fallen heroes". I studied the picture intently but could see no flaw so I confirmed with Levi that I definitely wanted to go ahead with the tattoo in the morning.

Only then did I turn my attention to the other tattoo designs on the table and was surprised to see that I was not the only guy with a mythological theme. Zac's design was of a naked Minotaur roaring at the viewer, it stood with legs outstretched, arms raised and fists clenched. It sported a gargantuan erection and low slung balls. Nathan's design was more classical showing two entwined naked warriors wrestling, one black one white and Marvin's was a lone wolf sitting on a rocky outcrop howling at a full moon high above it.

The six of us spent a lot of time discussing the tattoos and how they would be inked onto our backs and biceps, it sounded very daunting to me and for a couple of minutes I had real doubts about my courage to see the process through. I guess Sanun must have seen the doubt in my face for he gave me an affectionate hug and reassured me (and the others at the same time) that they were very experienced and had good stuff to take the pain away. I nodded my understanding and gave him a weary smile before doing an enormous yawn and nearly hitting Marvin in the mouth as I stretched.

"Right guys" Levi announced "it's getting late and you've had a tiring day so let's call it a day. Sanun has kindly set up the bathroom with plenty of towels for tonight and tomorrow morning. Oh, before I forget, tomorrow morning before you come down for breakfast please ensure that you're FULLY cleaned out. The reason will become apparent all too soon. Good night gentleman, if you need anything just ask, we'll be in the room next to you."

Having wished them both good night we made our way up to our room and set about making our beds. At this stage we felt it more appropriate to have single beds, for apart from the initiation ceremony we hardly knew each other and to share beds when we had partners back home didn't feel quite right somehow. Mind you, none of us were shy when it came to taking our clothes off, how could we when we had already seen each other naked and much more! So minutes later the four of us, giggling and totally starkers ran to the bathroom where we spent the next half an hour taking turns to shower, brush our teeth and have a shave. Admittedly it was a little crowded having four bodies in a room designed for no more than two but it did give an excuse for us to "accidently" bump into each other and get reacquainted with each other's buns and packets.

Later having made myself comfortable in my makeshift bed I thought about Kurt and wondered what he was doing and if he was thinking of me at all. I tossed and turned for what seemed like hours, but can really have only been half an hour or so because the last thing I heard before drifting off was the gentle snoring of Nathan in the next bed to me.

I woke the following morning to the sounds of movement in the room and quiet talking, opening my eyes a fraction I was in time to see Nathan, still naked with his back to me talking to Marvin who by now had a pair of pants on and was folding his blankets up. As I watched them Nathan bent down to pick his shorts up and in doing so allowed me full view of his balls swinging freely between his legs and I could just see them tip of his cock behind them. All too soon he pulled the shorts up and that was that, sighing I knew it was time for me to get up too. I sat up in bed trying to remember what I had done with my boxers last night. Damn! I'd been lazy and left them in the bathroom, so there was no option other than to remain naked until I got there. Okay, I could have gone to my bag and retrieved a clean pair but that seemed a waste as I had a feeling they would not be remaining on for long bearing in mind the events of my previous visit here and Levi's comments last night.

So wasting no time and ignoring the other's raised eyebrows I made my bed and sauntered off to the bathroom for the requested shower and deep clean out. I was soon joined by the other three and the banter between us resumed along much the same lines as the previous evening. As I was already naked and the first to finish with the shower it seemed logical that I would be the first to get cleaned out, however having looked around the bathroom I couldn't see a suitable douching appliance. With towel wrapped around my waist I left the others and went in search of our hosts. From the noises I could hear coming from downstairs I guessed breakfast was being prepared so I headed off in that direction.

"Morning Levi. Morning Sanun. Sorry to bother you just when you're both busy in the kitchen but...." I trailed off as they both turned around at the sound of my voice.

"Good morning Danny!" Levi responded with a smile "what can we do for you on this bright and sunny morning?"

"Well, last night you said about having a deep clean out before coming down for breakfast but I can't find the douching equipment anywhere. Am I missing something?" I asked.

"Sorry, that was my fault" Sanun said apologetically "I forgot to set it up before I went to bed!"

"Never mind, there'll be plenty of time after breakfast as we're nearly ready for it anyway. Would you mind calling the other's down please and tell them just to wear their towels as you are now" Levi instructed as he turned the bacon over under the grill.

"Sure thing" I replied and ran back up the stairs to tell the others to follow my lead.

Half an hour later all six of us were sitting round the breakfast table, two fully dressed the rest naked except for towels around our waists, tucking into a large fried breakfast. We were told to eat as much as we wanted so we did and cleared everything on the table! Sanun asked if we wanted anymore but we were completely full by then and raised our hands in surrender. We sat for a few minutes longer finishing off our fresh orange juices before Levi informed us it was time for us to be cleaned out. To save on time he had decided to do a group clean out in the back yard using the garden hose! I wondered what the neighbours might think but I needn't have worried for as we filed out into the back yard the building enclosed it on two sides with a thick hedge on third and the neighbour's garage wall enclosed the final side. There was no way anyone was going to look in on us unless they could climb buildings!

Levi told us to remove our towels and use them as kneeling pads as we got down on all fours, in a row, with our bums raised in the air. I was at one end of the row and as I looked over at the other three I gave them a wry smile as if to say we've been here before. Marvin, the nearest to me took the words right out of my mouth and then voiced the question as to why we needed to be cleaned out.

"All will be revealed in good time" Levi informed us "for now just enjoy yourselves and go with the flow. Think of it as a little holiday, for soon enough you will be going back to work and this will be a distant memory."

As he said this Sanun joined us carrying a small can of Crisco and proceeded to apply the grease to each of our holes in turn. I could tell from the way he applied the grease that he was experienced with this activity and wondered if he would slip me a finger or two when he got to me. I was sadly disappointed when he did for all I got was a small wad of grease pushed up inside me and grease smeared all around the rim before he stood up, job finished. Next came the garden hose, which was a bit of an exaggeration for all though that is what it had originally been it had since been adapted for its intended use as a douching tube. At one end was the familiar small metal butt plug with its many holes and the other was being carried into the kitchen to be attached to the mixer tap. After the temperature of the water had been adjusted to Levi's satisfaction Sanun then inserted the plug into my anus allowing my ring to grip tightly onto the plug's neck. Immediately I could feel the water flowing into me slowly filling my rectum with the tepid fluid. It wasn't long before I began to feel uncomfortable but before I could protest Levi reached underneath me and palpated my stomach enabling the water to flow further up in to me. When my stomach was fully distended the plug was pulled out and Sanun moved on to repeat the procedure with Marvin.

As for me, I made a dash to the open drain and quickly squatted over the hole just as the water and faeces mixture cascaded from my backside. I remained like that until I was sure that there was nothing more to come out. Standing to one side I watched with interest Marvin, Zac and Nathan undergo the same routine until we had all emptied the first load out. We then got back down on all fours and were filled up with water for a second time, and then a third. It was only on the fourth douching that Levi was satisfied that the exiting water was completely clean.

Halfway through I noticed that Sanun had disappeared indoors and hadn't returned which led me to wonder what he was up to but had no time to think much of it as I was still being cleaned out by Levi. However it became apparent as to what he had been doing when we returned from the yard carrying our towels over our shoulders. The living area had changed slightly, the table was still in the middle of the room but the dining chairs had been replaced by what looked like ergonomically designed stools with foot rests and the seat sloped slightly forwards. I noticed that each one had a screw thread hole in the centre. Mmmm I thought to myself as I studied them suspiciously. Just at that point Sanun entered the room carrying a large cardboard box and placed it down with a thump on the table. He beckoned us over and doing so we peered into the box. Inside were four large elongated butt plugs with metal screw threads sunk into the neck of each plug. There was also a large can of Crisco and rolls of tissue paper to wipe the grease off again afterwards.

Taking the lead I picked one of the butt plugs up, didn't matter which for they were all of the same size, about a foot long, as wide as my wrist at the tip and about as wide as my elbow at the flared base before narrowing to wrist size again for the neck.

"I take it these are meant for us?" I asked, already knowing the answer.

"Got it in one!" Levi said with a grin on his face "I'm not sure if you've been told about this, not only am I to tattoo each of you guys. I have also been tasked by the clan to not only maintain your anal capability but to increase it further until you are able to easily swallow an object the width of two fists and up to eighteen inches in length."

"But why that big? Surely a fist is more than enough! It was for the assessments" Nathan exclaimed.

"I have no idea why, I'm just doing as I'm instructed. The clan pays me handsomely and expects their requests to be carried out to the letter. You ought to bear that in mind young man" Levi said in a serious tone.

Needing no further encouragement I did what was obviously required which was to screw the butt plug onto to the stool. Once it was firmly in place I liberally greased it up using the Crisco from the can that Sanun had kindly opened for me. I went to take another load of the grease to apply to my backside when I heard a voice behind me say

"No allow me please. I need to gauge your capabilities before we go much further."

I turned around in time to see Levi scoop a large wad of the Crisco out of the can and play with it in his hands to warm it up.

"How would you like me?" I asked with a raised eyebrow.

"Oh, if you'd like to bend over the table with your chest resting on its surface. Then spread your legs and pull your cheeks apart that would be perfect" he said with a faint smile.

I just nodded and did as requested, as I reached behind me and pulled my cheeks apart I heard the quiet footfalls of the others walking round behind me and joining Levi to get a good view of the action. For the first time that I could remember I felt no embarrassment for being in such a compromising position, perhaps it was because of the company or the surroundings or both. Either way I just closed my eyes and focused on the attention my bum was receiving. First I felt Levi's fingers grease up my crack and then my anal ring before pushing inside the ball of softened grease. Taking slow breaths I relaxed and swallowed with ease the grease and the two fingers that were pushing it in. The fingers smeared the grease all around inside my rectum before withdrawing to be replaced by three fingers. I could tell from his deft and confident actions that he was a master at arse play which helped me to relax further and when he put four fingers I simply sighed in pleasure. He took his time and spent what felt like ages corkscrewing and pushing the fingers in and out of my willing hole. I felt so relaxed that I barely noticed when he withdrew, tucked his thumb behind his fingers forming a cone and slowly pushed them past my ring. As his hand got to the widest part I took another deep breath and pushed back on it driving the hand up into my rectum. I moaned quietly at the familiar and wonderfully full feeling that a fist always provided. Behind me I heard Levi and Sanun offer words of encouragement to me while I swear I heard Zac remark about how much he would like to bury his fist up my hole too.

"All in good time young man" Levi chuckled "business first, there will be plenty of time for fun later I promise."

With that he returned his attention to the task at hand, so to speak. Having left his hand motionless for a minute or two he slowly but surely pushed his fist further up my rectum until I felt his finger tips brushing my inner ring. He then repeated the same process with the inner ring as he had with the outer ring. Within a few minutes he had breached that barrier too and slid his fist deep into my bowels before sliding out of me with one smooth movement.

For a moment I stayed where I was and felt empty missing the intrusion, but was brought back to my senses when Levi slapped me on the arse and told me to stand up and allow Nathan to be assessed. As I did so Sanun beckoned me to join him round the other side of the dining table and pointed to the stool to which I had already attached the butt plug. I moved the stool nearer to the table and climbed on to it, standing on the foot bars I positioned myself until the point of the butt plug was just touching my hole. As both my stretched out hole and the plug were liberally greased up I had no difficulty at all fully impaling myself. My ring gently closed around the neck and as it did so I looked across the table in time to see Levi's fist slowly disappear between Nathan's tanned cheeks and up into his rectum. Nathan met my gaze and although his hazel eyes were slightly glazed and beads of sweat appeared across his brow he still smiled broadly. I asked him if he was okay and he nodded in response before looking over his shoulder to watch Levi slide further inside him.

Within a few minutes Nathan had been assessed and was sitting on the stool next to me, impaled by the butt plug of course. Like me his cock was semi-erect from being constantly aroused by the intruder. Zac was next and I began to suspect that he was a bit of a show off, for having seen how Nathan and I had acted, he appeared determined to go one better. As he assumed the position bent over the table and spread his cheeks wide he grinned at us and threw a wink before actively backing onto Levi's fist. Then having swallowed the fist in record time he looked over his shoulder and said that he could easily take another.

"I'm sure you could Zac" Levi replied drily "but as I've already explained to you, this session is purely business not for personal gratification. Now turn round and let me carry on with my assessment."

Crestfallen Zac did as he was told, much to our amusement, and let Levi do as he wished inside him. I felt a little uneasy sitting here watching Zac with his ringlets covering his face, for I felt some attraction to him beyond his handsomeness. Deliberately I looked away from him and over at Marvin who was waiting nervously for his turn at the table.

Fifteen minutes later all four of us were now sitting impaled on our stools around the dining table awaiting guidance on what was to follow next. We didn't have long to wait, maybe ten minutes or so, Levi re-entered the living room dressed in what to me looked like a surgical gown, cap and mask. Sanun followed close behind him wearing regular jeans and a T-shirt carrying a hold all bag. He placed it on the table and retrieved what can only be described as an adult's activity set. There were packs of playing cards, laptop computers, DVDs, video game discs, the latest issues of men's (gay and straight) magazines all of which we were free to use as we please Sanun informed us.

Before that though we had to decide who was having the first session of the tattoo inking done, so we drew straws with the shortest going first and the longest last. Marvin drew the shortest so he was led off through the front of the shop into the small tattoo studio. I felt a little sorry him as he had looked so nervous, not knowing what to expect, but with words of encouragement from Sanun he had painted a brave smile on his face as he followed Levi out of the room. I had drawn the second shortest straw, so I would be next followed by Nathan and then finally Zac.

As for the rest of us it was simply a case of being patient and waiting for our turn, all the time sitting impaled on the elongated butt plug. The only time we were allowed off the stool was to relieve ourselves using the downstairs toilet, food and drink was brought to us at the table, we just had to ask for it. Sanun really was a sweet guy, nothing was too much trouble and he always showed us a friendly smile. At first we played several games of poker using match sticks for money but that soon lost its novelty as we realised to our cost that Nathan was an excellent poker player. The laptops became the next favourite time killer, as for me I surfed the internet and caught up on emails that I had received over the last couple of weeks and never got the chance to pick up.

After about an hour and a half Levi returned and told me to follow him. I got off the stool rather stiffly and the plug left my arse with a squelchy plop and I felt the melted Crisco and body juices trickle down my leg – Yuk! Quickly I snatched some of the tissue from off the table and wiped myself clean giving the others a rueful smile as I did so. As they say, what goes up must come down. I followed him into the shop, where to my surprise I spotted Marvin laying face down on a large blanket in the middle of the floor. His back and the tops of his arms were covered in cling film and on top of those a couple of hand towels. Other than that he was still completely naked.

I went over to greet him and ask how it went but before I got there Levi told me that I was wasting my breath for he was unconscious and it would be another hour or so before he woke up. It was at this point I began to feel panicky and not so sure I wanted to have the tattoos done having seen the state of Marvin! Too late, Levi took me by the elbow and steered me in the direction of the tattoo studio. Closing the door behind him he gestured me to climb into the chair, which looked like a cross between a massage couch and a dentist's chair. I climbed onto the arched padded surface face down and rested my forearms on the suspended arm rests beneath. Before I could react Levi had secured both my arms to the arm rests using the attached leather cuffs effectively pinning me down.

I looked at him in alarm but with a reassuring smile he said this was to simply prevent me from moving around when the needles started to ink me. He then cuffed my ankles too, again for the same reason apparently. Another surprise lay in wait for me, the chair's lower half swung open as Levi turned a wheel spreading my legs wide open. The explanation was that it gave him easier access to my lower back when he was inking the blood trickling down between my cheeks. I would have shrugged my shoulders if I could have so all I could do was lay there waiting for the ordeal to start.

Levi hung up my tattoo design on the wall in front of me and then offered me a cigarette. I shook my head saying that I didn't smoke, only to be told that it was one of his 'special' smokes like I had when I got waxed. Mmm that memory was still painful for me, but if Levi was offering it to me then I guessed that it was a good idea. So I nodded instead and agreed to smoke one before we began. He lit it before placing it between my lips and I inhaled the pungent smoke, at first I choked but as I grew accustomed to it I inhaled deeper and the effects increased dramatically. The room spun and my vision blurred into a kaleidoscope of distorted colours, I giggled despite myself and when Levi said he was going to start inking I just didn't care.

Oh shit! The pain! As the needles lanced my skin injecting their ink it felt like a red hot knife was being scraped across and through my skin. Still puffing on the cigarette I groaned despite myself and sucked even harder on it desperate to deaden the pain further. Slowly, ever so slowly the needles moved across my shoulders, time stood still for me as I tried to ignore the pain. Taking a break Levi offered me another cigarette which I gratefully accepted and smoked as he resumed inking my shoulders. By the time I had finished the second cigarette I was almost unconscious but I still could not ignore the pain coming from my lower back. As he outlined the blood trickling down my spine I could bear it no longer and asked for Levi to stop.

"I can't stop now" Levi replied "I still have your biceps to outline and the remainder of the blood flow."

"I'm sorry but I really can't cope with the pain any longer. Perhaps another cigarette might help?" I asked trying to keep the desperation out of my voice that I felt inside.

"No, you can't have more than two otherwise you will be sick. The only alternative I can offer is a morphine-based anaesthetic which will need to be anally administered for safest and quickest effect. Do I have your permission to administer it?"

"Yes! I need something, anything, to take the pain away."

"Okay, I will prepare the solution and administer it before continuing" he reassured me.

I heard him walk out of the room and within a couple of minutes he had returned, a little too quickly for him to have made anything up, he must have had it ready and waiting for me. Just as he had done with Marvin I suspected. I heard him step up behind me and almost immediately I felt the cold metallic nozzle of a syringe press against my anus and slide easily into my rectum. The fluid quickly flowed into me, it wasn't long before I felt woozy and then the lights went out in my brain.

Slowly, ever so slowly consciousness came back to me. First I felt coldness in my arms and feet, then a dull ache across my back and shoulders before a wave of nausea hit my stomach. Groaning in discomfort I opened my eyes and looked around me. The view looked wrong to me, everything seemed very tall and distorted and I could see two dark shapes nearby. Then I heard it, a dentist's drill. No scrub that as I remembered where I was, it was the tattooist's inking needles at work, presumably on Zac as I recognised his voice whimpering in pain.

"Danny, are you awake yet?"

"Uh I think so. Is that you Marvin?" I asked groggily.

"Yes. How are you doing?" he asked as he crawled over to me, wrapped in the blanket he had been lying on earlier.

"Sore and sick" I replied sitting up unsteadily.

"Me too, but the sickness has gone now the anaesthetic has worn off, thankfully."

I made no response as I hugged my knees up to my chest, wincing as the movement pulled the cling film on the traumatised skin on my back and biceps. Muttering to myself I rested my head on my knees wondering not for the first time why I was putting myself through this torture.

"Here, let me put a blanket around you otherwise you're gonna get cold" Marvin said taking charge of the situation.

There was no resistance from me and I smiled gratefully at him as he wrapped me up in a spare blanket he had found from somewhere. He sat close to me in a comfortable silence while we watched and waited for Nathan to stir from his anaesthetic induced slumber. Before long I heard a door open and saw Levi carrying the unconscious body of Zac. He gently laid Zac onto the fourth blanket, put a pillow beneath his head and towels over his shoulders. He checked Nathan quickly before squatting down next to us and asked if we felt well enough to join him and Sanun for some afternoon tea out in the backyard.

We confirmed that we were, I for one felt very dehydrated and asked for water rather than tea. I let the other two lead the way as I was still a little wobbly on my feet but didn't want them fussing over me. Waiting for us in the other room was Sanun with drinks and a round of sandwiches plus a couple of painkillers for each of us. It felt good to be sitting out in the sun letting the sun's rays warming up my chilled and naked body. As I drank the tall glass of iced water and ate my ham sandwiches, Sanun inspected my tattoos and removed the cling film from them. He wiped the dried blood away with some antiseptic wipes. He expressed admiration of Levi's work (well he would, of course!) before rubbing soothing cream into my reddened skin before covering them over again with the towels. He advised me to keep them covered to prevent further skin irritation.

The rest of the afternoon was spent lounging around waiting for Nathan and Zac to join us again. That evening having had cooling showers and finally been allowed to put some shorts on, we inspected each other's tattoos now that the skin had lost some of its redness. I had to admit although the designs were simply line drawings at this stage the overall pictures could be seen and I thought they were all going to be striking when completed.

Chapter 4 – Late night entertainment

Later that night as I laid in bed, I tried to ignore the dread building up inside me, knowing that we still had several days of the inking to endure. Sleep would not come to me. I felt very alone being separated from Kurt and by now the others were fast asleep. Or so I thought. A slight scraping sound caught my attention, looking in the direction of the sound I saw Zac crawling out of his bed and moving in my direction.

"What are you up to?" I whispered trying not to wake Nathan who was snoring quietly in the bed next to me.

"I'm lonely. Can I have a cuddle please?" he whispered back.

"Uh, I guess so but why me?" I replied feeling uneasy with the situation.

"You're the only one who's awake" he said matter of factly.

"Okay, cuddle up but watch the tattoos please" I said rolling over to one side to make room for him.

"Will do, thanks" he grinned as he crawled in behind me.

I felt the heat of his body lying next to me and despite myself I felt a gravitational pull towards him. Zac must have felt it too for he shifted his position until his lower half pressed against mine, being careful not to touch my back or shoulders. This had the effect of pushing his packet into my bum which against my better judgement I responded by pushing back on to him. He took this as a signal of my acceptance and with one hand stroked himself to erection before sliding it along my crack between my cheeks. As his cockhead slid over my anus I felt a surge of lust wash over me and under my breath I asked him to fuck me.

I heard a gentle chuckle and "I thought you'd never ask" whispered into my ear. He scooted down the bed until his face pressed against my cheeks, instinctively I pulled them apart to give him easier access. Sure enough as they parted he pushed his face closer and stuck his tongue out. This was no gentle tease of my hole as Kurt had done in the past. Zac appeared to have only one goal in mind and that was to apply as much saliva to my hole as possible. Not that I minded for the sensations I was experiencing were heavenly and could have laid like this forever with my arse being ridden by his face!

Zac's need to thrust his cock up me proved too great for the rimming to last for long. Taking hold of my hips he rotated them until I was lying on my front with my legs spread wide. Placing his hands carefully on either side of my chest to support himself he climbed on top of me with his cock pressing between my cheeks. With one hand I reached behind me and took hold of his cock and guided its head to my back door. Needing no encouragement he increased the pressure until his cock slipped inside (okay it didn't take that much pressure given the stretching it had had today). There was still plenty of grease inside me so his decent sized cock was able to move around inside me so smoothly and easily that I felt no discomfort even though he didn't wait for me to adjust to his presence.

Although sex with Kurt could be animalistic and rough at times, it was always done with mutual love and pleasure but with Zac it was all about him. Yes, he was certainly experienced at fucking and could do it very well but not once did he check with me to see if I was enjoying it (which I was, but that's not the point). Smoothly and continuously he thrust in an out of me slowly increasingly the speed and force he used until I was grunting with each bang into me. Getting close to orgasm he too became more vocal and by the time he came to a shuddering halt, sending his jism into me, he was grunting "fuck that ass" with each stroke.

Falling silent after his orgasm he pulled out of me and rolled off panting heavily. More than a little frustrated that my needs hadn't been catered for, I took the initiative by quickly grabbing hold of his legs and bringing them up and back against his chest. The look for surprise on his face was comical but I took no notice for I was concentrating more on his anus which was now gaping slightly because of the position he was in.

"Perfect, now it's my turn" I said in an authoritive tone to my voice.

With one hand I held his thighs in position, with the other I spat on my fingers and used them to lubricate his slightly greasy hole. Give him his due Zac got into the role of bottom very quickly, offering me words of encouragement before using his own hands he felt for his hole and used his fingers to stretch it wider for me. Oh how I wished I had a camera for his anus was gaping so wide and open I could have shot my load there and then, which would have been a waste! So before I lost control I quickly shoved my rock hard cock into the waiting hole and buried it up to the hilt in one thrust, bringing a satisfying grunt from Zac. By now I could hear sounds of movement from the other two guys, not surprisingly our antics had woken them up.

I had expected complaints and angry comments from them but nothing verbal came our way. Instead actions spoke louder than words as the saying goes. I was caught off guard when I felt a couple of fingers slide between my cheeks and explore my crack. Ever the gent I stopped thrusting into Zac to allow the fingers to go where they wanted, which apparently was my anus. Being greasy and jism coated my hole opened up wide, eager to let them in.

As the two fingers felt around inside me I heard the familiar voice of Marvin murmur in my ear "gonna let me in?"

"Uh huh" was all I said in response.

Nothing else was required so Marvin knelt down beside me and started to play with my hole in earnest. Quite swiftly the two fingers became three, then four and all too soon I felt his fingers form a cone with the thumb tucked in behind. With only a little bit of effort and a grunt from me his fist slipped inside where he held it stationary for a moment to allow me adjust to the intrusion. Once comfortable I started to fuck Zac and at the same time fuck myself on his fist, now that really was heaven! I wondered where Nathan was but as I looked up I saw him sitting on Zac's face receiving an enthusiastic rim. Quickly Nathan became erect and changed positions, thrusting his cock into Zac's open mouth and down his willing throat. Now that we were all awake we felt we could make all the noise we liked, which was a mistake because after a few minutes the bedroom door opened and the light flicked on.

"What the hell is going on......" Levi's voice boomed but trailed off as he took in the view.

"Oh my God!" Sanun cried out camply "I was only joking when I said it sounded like an orgy going on next door. I didn't think you were actually having one!"

The four of us were frozen to the spot and judging by Levi's expression it was comical for he went from scowling to chuckling within a minute.

"This guys, gives me an idea which I need to explore with Owen before I put it into action. Do me a favour please and cool it, you'll have plenty of opportunities to have some fun later as I've already promised" he said with hands on hips.

The magic of our session had disappeared and it was actually rather embarrassing being caught in the act like a naughty boy. My first thought was of Kurt. Guilt washed over me but I dismissed it as being a pointless emotion for neither of us had ever discussed fidelity since we had got together. Living with the clan didn't lend itself to monogamy and it might even be destructive in the long term. We simultaneously disengaged and avoided their eye contact as we filed past our two hosts in the direction of the bathroom.

The next few days followed a similar pattern to our first day here. We'd get up, wash and shave before cleaning ourselves out in the bathroom now that Sanun had set up the douching hose. Then wearing just a towel around our waists we'd have breakfast before one by one we had another session in the tattoo studio where our tattoos were coloured in stages. While we waited for our turn in the studio we were required to impale ourselves on the butt plugs to continue the stretching of our rectums and anal rings. Each morning we would find that they had been replaced by new ones that were a couple of inches longer and half an inch wider than the previous ones.

By mutual agreement Levi ceased offering us his 'special' cigarettes and simply administered the anaesthetic anally, which must have been a stronger dose because we didn't wake up again until evening. Although it made the days seem shorter at least we were spared the agony of enduring the hour long sessions of inking!

It was on the evening of day five that Levi announced that the inking sessions had finished and the tattoos were now complete. All that remained to be done was for a photo shoot tomorrow morning followed by a video session in the afternoon. In the meantime our skin was going to be allowed to calm down overnight, assisted by a cream Sanun applied to our backs and shoulders which soothed and sealed the ink into skin. When questioned as to what the video session was going to involve Levi wouldn't be drawn, all he would disclose was that he was delivering on a promise.

Day six dawned overcast and rainy, not the best way to start our last day with Levi and Sanun, but neither would be daunted by the inclement weather. Levi had wanted to set up the photo shoot in the back yard but this was not possible so the set was erected in our bedroom once our clutter had been cleared to one end of the room. We spent a very tedious couple of hours in front of the camera. Levi had us posing singly and in groups, sometimes wearing just our jeans and sometimes naked for close up and distance shots. Now I know why I never wanted to become a professional model. Well that and the fact I wasn't handsome enough!

By the time we had finished the photo shoot and a welcome lunch the clouds had blown away and the sun was rapidly evaporating the water pooled on the back yard. Levi cheered up immensely and like an excited teenager set up a sun lounger against the brick wall in the bright sunshine. While he was doing this Sanun disappeared momentarily to return casually holding a video camera and stood to one side activating it and adjusting its settings.

Levi stood in front of the camera and started speaking into it introducing himself as the producer, Sanun as the cameraman and the four of us as the cast. Cast? I thought to myself, cast in what? Sometimes I can be so dense! Obviously we were going to be filmed but doing what? Then it hit me like an express train.... Levi had promised that we would enjoy ourselves once the tattoos had been completed, perhaps that moment was now. Looking around at my companions I could see from their expressions that they had reached the same conclusion.

Once Levi was satisfied with his speech he nodded to Sanun who then panned the camera on us, catching us off guard as we stood casually by the doorway with hands in our pockets. Out of view of the camera Levi gestured for me to walk over to the sun lounger, spread out the rolled up towel before stripping naked and laying face down to do some sunbathing. Being careful not to look at the camera directly I did as I was instructed, behaving as casually as possible. After removing my jeans and T-shirt I stood there in my boxers for a moment facing into the sun with eyes closed enjoying its warmth. Then slipping my fingers into the shorts waistband I slowly pushed them down before stepping out of them and laying face down on the lounger with my back to the camera. I rested my head on my hands and closed my eyes feigning sleep.

I heard footsteps close to me and by the way they moved around me I guessed it was Sanun focussing on various aspects of my body. Then as he stepped away I heard more footsteps approaching, curious I opened my eyes and looked over my shoulder to see Zac sauntering over, already naked and stroking himself to erection with one hand and carrying a tube of lube in the other. He nodded towards my bum so I obediently spread my legs until they were hanging over either side of the lounger with my feet resting on the ground. Having climbed on board he knelt down between my legs and proceeded to give me the same style rimming that he had last night. Out of the corner of my eye I discretely watched Sanun film us from all angles while Levi was instructing the others off screen.

Before long I felt Zac's tongue withdraw to be replaced moments later by his hard cock, again like last night he spared me no feeling by shoving his cock up me in one quick thrust. Rather theatrically I reared up and cried out in pain and shock (in reality it was neither) for the benefit of the camera. Zac took no notice of me at all for he was totally absorbed in providing a good show for the camera and fucking the life out of my backside. Unfortunately for him the excitement of it all tipped him over the edge a little too soon and with a cry he collapsed on top of me as his hips came to a shuddering halt and he shot pulse after pulse of jism into me. He stayed there for a couple of minutes catching his breath before slipping out of me and disappearing to wash off his cock.

Marvin was my next visitor but unlike last night he didn't go to fist me, instead he flipped me over onto my back and fucked me missionary style. As he was doing so, Nathan climbed onto the sun lounger and lubed up Marvin's anus, finger fucking him while Marvin fucked me. After a couple minutes of this Nathan pushed Marvin forward a little and then slid his cock easily up the willing hole. Marvin was now the meat in our sandwich and from his expression I could tell he loved it! Moments later the milk chocolate globes of Zac's cheeks descended on my upturned face, pulled apart by his hands to allow me easier access to his puckered pink hole. As he squatted lower and lower I opened my mouth and stuck my tongue out ready to lick the quivering ring. As my own ring received a pounding so I polished and lapped at the ring now being slowly impaled on my tongue. I had never done this before and the smells and tastes took some getting used to I have to admit, but being the slut that I am, I just got on with enjoying the experience. From the sighs of contentment above me I guessed that Zac was enjoying it too.

This situation lasted until I felt Marvin's cock pulse before sending yet more jism deep into my rectum. As Marvin pulled out Zac stood up and welcome fresh air blew over both my face and along my crack. I made to sit up but found that I was pinned down by my legs, held in position against my chest by Zac who had remained astride my head. Glancing up I could see his balls and semi flaccid cock hanging just inches from my face, so near and yet so far.

Peering between my open legs I watched Nathan climb back onto the sun lounger and kneel down before my exposed backside. Peering over Nathan's shoulder I spotted Sanun hold the camera out to get a clear view of my hole, again I had to concentrate on not looking at the camera. I could just make out the figure of Marvin standing nearby holding out an opened can of Crisco. Nathan scooped out a handful of the white grease, rolled it into a ball and then pushed it into my rectum. Taking another handful he thoroughly greased up both his hands and started to massage my anal ring with his finger tips. He took his time in doing so, warming and relaxing my ring with gentle swirling motions gradually pushing them further in as he did so. Then as I took a deep breath and relaxed I felt a hand slide past my ring and up my rectum until it encountered my inner ring. To take my mind off the intrusion I looked up to see that Zac was still standing over me and an idea occurred to me. I called Marvin over and asked him to pass me the can of Crisco, grinning he did so and held it out for me. I scooped out a handful of the grease and set about smearing it along Zac's crack, surprised by my action he yelped before chuckling and spread his legs wider to give me easier access.

I fed more grease into his anus using two fingers, then inserting a third finger I smeared the softening grease all around the inside of his rectum. Zac was clearly happy with this intrusion for he started rising and falling on my fingers, grinning to myself I coned my fingers and held them up to meet his descending anus. As he sank down I pushed up and to my amazement he swallowed my fist in one go, okay he groaned loudly from the sudden intrusion but he made no attempt to pull away. By now Nathan had pushed the whole of his fist past my inner ring and I was beginning to feel very full and rather uncomfortable. I made the mistake of asking Marvin how far had Nathan gone as he replied with a stunned tone to his voice.

"Oh! Ah, his elbow has just disappeared from view and he's slid in another inch!"

"Holy shite!" I replied, not sure if I should be proud or scared.

"Danny, how much more can you take?" Zac asked as he impaled himself further onto my fist.

"Aaargh! No more please, it's almost hurting now......" I gasped.

Levi gestured for us to disengage and once we had wiped ourselves clean we were to sit on the sun lounger and wait for further instructions. Sanun in the meantime kept recording us until we were sitting down, still naked and smiling at the camera. He then turned the camera onto Levi who did a brief explanatory speech about the next activity, which was apparently to prove to the clan that we had met their required anal capacity and that Levi had done his job successfully.

Levi walked indoors followed closely by Sanun and returned a moment later carry what for all the world looked like four clear open ended plastic test tubes the size of fire extinguishers! Grinning in our direction Levi placed them on the ground in a row evenly spaced, upright with the flared open end on the ground. He then told us to grease them up and see who would be the first to be sitting on the ground with the tube fully inserted up their rectums. We looked at one in shock for a moment before I pointed out that in terms of width the tubes were no larger than two fists and the same length as our forearms, so we should be able to accommodate them with a little bit of effort.

They nodded in agreement as they thought on my words before we stood up en masse and stepped over to the tubes and liberally greased them up using the Crisco offered to us. I guess that I and perhaps Zac had an unfair advantage over the other two as we had already been warmed up, so to speak. As I squatted down over the greasy plastic tube and aimed my hole at it I let my weight push it inside me. Crossing my legs I adopted a meditation position which helped guide it straight up inside and past my inner ring. Being so smooth it actually felt more comfortable than the fist had earlier and I experienced a bit of a head trip as my cheeks finally touched the ground and its flared base. Satisfied with my accomplishment I looked around me to watch the progress of the others, Zac the most competitive was just behind me and within a couple of minutes was sitting on the ground too. Marvin and Nathan were struggling however to get the tube past their inner rings, so needed Levi to help them with a mixture of relaxation coaching and his weight to help push them downwards.

Finally all four of us were sitting cross legged on the ground, looking a little red faced and sweaty from the effort, in front of a very happy looking Levi. Our next task was to kneel down on the ground as we had when receiving the douching hose for Sanun to inspect the insertions. Very carefully and with one hand behind us to ensure the tubing remained inside us we crouched down with our bums up in the air. For the next ten minutes we stayed like that as Levi went along the row with Sanun inserted his arm into the tube to demonstrate how far in he could go for the benefit of the camera. With a sigh of relief from us we were allowed to release the tubes and rest our bums for the remainder of the day.

Evening was a quiet affair as this was our last day and we all felt a little sad that our 'holiday' was nearly over, but at least we did have some good reminders of the stay in the form of tattoos and a DVD which Levi was busy copying and putting labels on ready for us to take back to the clan tomorrow.

The following morning we left just before sunrise having bid an emotional farewell to Levi and Sanun with loads of bear hugs and kisses all round. We thanked them for everything no end of times until it got a little embarrassing so with arms out of the window waving and a couple of toots on the car horn we started our journey back to the clan in Gettysburg.

The journey home seemed faster perhaps it was because we were keen to be with our partners again. I for one couldn't wait to hold Kurt again in my arms and receive his rib crushing hugs! We only stopped twice in the whole journey, both times to empty our bladders and once to feed our empty stomachs. As it was we didn't reach the rally site until early afternoon so it was still in full swing and crowded with visitors.

We parted company after I parked my car behind our trailer. It was hardly an emotional farewell as we all lived in neighbouring trailers but we still gave each other hugs and a kiss on the cheek before going our separate ways. I couldn't wait to hit the shower as even I could smell the sweat on me as it had been very hot in the car on the way down and the sun was still very strong in the sky.

Half an hour later I felt a million times better, refreshed and smelling of aftershave, wearing just a pair of jeans and my work boots. Yep, have gone commando to give Kurt a kick when he grabs my packet, he likes to remind me that I'm his. No top today, I want to show off my new tattoos to everyone as I am so proud of them. As I locked the trailer door behind me I sauntered off in the direction of the crowds with hands in my pockets. I tried to look as masculine and casual as possible to disguise the fact that I felt just a little bit nervous not knowing if Kurt had missed me as much as I had him.

I needn't have worried because he spotted me before I saw him and immediately came running over with a great big grin on his face calling out my name. Startled I turned to face the sound just in time to be swept off my feet and crushed against his chest in a vice-like hug. Releasing me he hungrily kissed my lips, not caring who saw, before taking a step back to take a good look at me.

"You sure have changed!" he said with a satisfied smile on his face.

"Oh, just a little bit, glad you've noticed" I replied drily.

He didn't respond for he was too intent on studying the clan tattoo on my right bicep which read 'Danny cub of Kurt 2012'. With a satisfied nod he walked round me, first examining the two intertwined snakes within the Greek motifs on my left bicep before turning his attention to the Medusa killing Perseus tattoo on my back. I heard him whistle in appreciation of the artwork and said that he thought Levi deserved a bonus for doing such a good job. I had to agree with him on that because judging by the reaction of other people around me they too had found the tattoos awe inspiring. Whether it was the artwork or the subject matter I didn't know nor really care.

I spent the remainder of the afternoon working alongside Kurt and I'm sure that on more than one occasion I caught him watching me thoughtfully. I stored this away in my brain for discussion later once we were alone. At long last the final stragglers departed leaving the rally site deserted except for the clan members and rally crew. With practised efficiency we cleared up all the litter ready for us to de-camp in the morning.

Back in the trailer we headed straight for the shower and wasted no time in washing off the say's sweat and grime, throughout which Kurt had a distinctly lustful look in his eye which needed no translation! I had let Kurt go first (well he is my bear after all and I am just the cub) to give him time to tidy up the bedroom and prepare himself for me joining him there. Except that having kept the bedroom tidy he had nothing to do but wait for me impatiently, stoking himself to erection with a grin on his face. I had barely had time to towel myself dry when he took matters into his own hands and literally pushed me into the bedroom and closed the door behind us.

I sat down on the bed with my legs spread and beckoned him over, as he stepped up to me I wrapped my arms around his thighs pulling him closer still until his stomach was pressing against my face. I gave it an affectionate nibble before kissing my way down his body until I had reached his cock which was now rock hard and bobbing with excitement. Taking his cockhead in my mouth I lovingly licked and sucked on it drawing a sigh from Kurt, who then rested his hands on the top of my head and gently pushed downwards. Taking the hint I opened my mouth wide and relaxed my throat. Bobbing my head up and down I took an ever increasing length of his cock into my mouth until I was fully impaled on his shaft and my chin was pressing against his balls. Taking control Kurt held my head still while he fucked my mouth, not caring if I was controlling my breathing for the need in him was too great to hold back.

Half choking half loving it I savoured his cock pistoning in and out, it was great to be back where I belonged. All too soon I heard Kurt make a keening cry and with a final thrust he exploded sending jism down my throat and into my stomach. Bucking and shuddering he remained where he was until his ejaculations had ceased and with a heartfelt sigh he pulled his softening cock from my mouth still oozing its slimy contents. I wouldn't let him go until I had licked his cock clean and sucked out the last of his juices. I looked up at him and he looked down at me, each of us mirroring the other's happy expression.

Together we climbed onto the bed and for several minutes we lay spooned together confessing how much we had missed each other. It wasn't long before I felt Kurt's erection press into the small of my back and then he shifted his position as he guided it between my cheeks. Twisting my head round I kissed him before reaching over for the tube of KY on my bedside cabinet. Taking it from me Kurt said "Allow me" before lubing up his cock and then liberally lubing my hole inside and out.

His cockhead pressed against my ring before pushing past and straight up my rectum in one smooth steady thrust. Unlike the previous times when he had hurt me doing this impatient insertion, now I could accept the impalement quite comfortably and even pushed back further grinding my bum into his hips.

"That's my boy!" Kurt encouraged "I knew Levi would expand on your abilities while you stayed with him."

"Oh yes, he did that all right!" I replied remembering the over sized test tube.

He fell silent after that as he concentrated on cramming as much of his cock into me as he possibly could. Deciding that spooning wasn't the best position for this he rolled me over onto my stomach cock still in me, and laid on top, winding me in the process. Not noticing this fact he continued to fuck me, this time driving his cock further into me drawing grunts from me each time he did so. It didn't take long for him to cum again but I still had a raging hard on and no method of relief. Perhaps aware of this he climbed off and out of me, flipped me onto my back before applying KY to his own anus.

I watched him with surprise as his sat astride me and impaled himself on my erection. I had thought him acting as bottom had been a one off for the post initiation celebration, clearly this was not the case as he rose and fell on my shaft with enthusiasm. Unable to contain myself I shot my load into him after only perhaps a dozen strokes, much to my chagrin.

Later sitting on the sofa watching yet another soccer match I suddenly remembered that I still had to resolve the problem about my job back in Glen Falls. The thought of which spoilt an otherwise perfect evening and I frowned to myself as I mulled over my options. Logan sitting opposite me laughed at my expression and made a comment about me looking like a bulldog chewing on a wasp. That did at least make me smile. Kurt had been totally absorbed in the soccer but the sound of Logan's voice did eventually get through to him and as he glanced from me to Logan and back to me again he asked.

"Eh? What did I miss?"

"Oh nothing really" I replied snuggling deeper into his shoulder before continuing "I was just wondering about my old job and what I was going to do about it."

"Nothing" he replied as he returned his attention back to the TV.

"Nothing? I can't just disappear and not say anything" I replied.

Sighing Kurt spoke to me slowly and loudly as if I was an idiot (no comments are required, thank you).

"You don't have to do anything because I've already sorted it. Like I've told you before, you're my cub and it's my duty to take care of this sort of thing. Now can I watch the rest of this match in peace please?"

"Yes Sir!" Logan and I replied in unison, the subject was clearly closed.

The following morning it seemed that life was back to normal, as if I had never been away. Having joined the others packing up the rally I found it hard to believe that I had only met Kurt just over six weeks ago and been with the clan for about a month. Already I was beginning to forget what my mundane life had been like prior to Kurt.

My former life was about to come crashing back in the form of a phone call. It was just before we stopped for lunch that my mobile rang with Perry on the other end. Surprised by the timing of his call, for he seldom contacted me until late evening, I asked him what was up. It was like a dam bursting and with barely a pause for breath he told me how after a night out in town he and Lewis had been held up at knife point by a gang of five thugs. During which they were robbed and had their wallets and mobile phones stolen. Ever since then they had been receiving menacing letters and phone calls warning them to get out of town and threatening them with violence if they didn't. I was stunned by what he had said and it took a minute or so to gather my thoughts before I started asking him questions about the contents of the letters and what they said during the calls.

With reluctance he told me about the homophobic nature of the communications and the way the thugs had acted towards him and Lewis. I was still having trouble reconciling what he was telling me with my longstanding memories of Glen Falls when a little warning bell rang in the back of my mind. I asked him to describe what the thugs looked like and the warning bell rang even louder. I gestured to Kurt to sit next to me and put the phone on loud speaker so that he could hear what Perry was telling me. He clearly shared my concern judging by his expression and the way his body stiffened as the conversation continued. Then as if he had made a decision his whole manner relaxed before he took the phone from me and spoke directly to Perry.

In a calm authoritive voice he told Perry to pack up his bags and be ready to leave tonight. He also told him to make sure that Lewis had done the same and that they stay together until we arrived. Having emphasised this point a couple of times he terminated the call before handing the phone back to me and rising to his feet pulling me up with him. The next half an hour flew past in a whirl of activity as Kurt organised a small posse to join us on our rescue mission. With Owen's permission we left Gettysburg taking three trucks with us and six clan members for support.

How we didn't get stopped by the police I don't know, for what should have been nearly a seven hour journey was done in five with only one stop to change over drivers. We pulled up outside Perry's house just before 19:00hrs dwarfing the neighbour's vehicles with our three trucks. Kurt jumped down from the driver's seat and bounded over to the front door using the doorbell rather than bang on the door as he would normally have done. The net curtains upstairs twitched and I spotted a nervous Perry looking down at us. I climbed out of the truck and made an exaggerated wave to gain his attention so he would realise that friends had arrived. Recognising me he grinned and looked over his shoulder, I saw his lips moving and within a couple of seconds the front door was flung open revealing a very relieved Lewis.

Kurt and I went inside while the other clan members parked the trucks around the corner to prevent unwanted attention being focussed on the house. A few minutes later they joined us inside where we heard in detail all about what had happened to Lewis and Perry during and after their meeting with the gang. As the tale unfolded and the homophobic driven violence used became apparent the mood in the room changed to one charged with anger. Kurt stood to one side and then announced that simply rescuing my best friends was not enough. These thugs needed to be taught a few lessons otherwise they would do it to other innocent guys who might not be so lucky. This was met with enthusiastic agreement, I realised that not all gay guys are scared of violence. In fact Kurt and these guys seemed to enjoy using their fists when there was a justifiable excuse.

Chapter 8 – The trap is sprung

Over a second mug coffee they sat down to work out a plan for finding the thugs and what was a suitable punishment. However the plan never came to fruition for the thugs in question decided to pay us a visit, what a mistake it proved to be for them. In the middle of the discussions there was a deafening bang on the door followed by several more bangs and a voicing shouting.

"Open this fucking door you fucking poofs. Don't try to hide I heard you talking!"

"Mmm nice guy" I whispered to Lewis trying to make light of the situation.

"Come on. Don't make it fucking worse for yourselves. We politely told you to get out of town. You haven't so now we're going to fucking help you" he voice snarled through the letterbox before banging on the door again.

Kurt and the clan members glanced at one another gesturing hiding points along the hallway and living room. Kurt then whispered into Perry's ear telling him to open the front door and then quickly withdraw to the living room before the thugs could grab hold of him. Lewis and I were to remain in the kitchen and arm ourselves with knives just in case things got out of hand. Nodding in compliance I mouthed to Kurt to be careful. Grinning in response he took up position behind the living room door and waited for Perry to bait the trap.

The plan worked perfectly, I heard Perry open the door to a jubilant cry from the thug on the other side of the door before it turned to a sound of frustration. Perry stepped backwards out of reach making placating noises which only served to increase their sense of power over their 'victim'. I could hear "come on lads let's get him" followed by multiple footfalls moving towards the living room. Suddenly their cries of triumph dwindled to "oh shits" and then cries of pain could be heard. By now the clan member's fists must have been making contact with their bodies judging by the "oofs" I could hear. The trap had been sprung and punishment meted out. There was silence for a minute before a couple of the clan members returned rubbing their knuckles asking for a knife, rope and old sheets.

Puzzled Perry did as he was told quickly returning from his utility room with the required items. Intrigued we followed the men back into the living room and saw the unconscious bodies of the five thugs piled on top of one another surrounded by seven very happy guys. Even so they kept a watchful eye on them in case they regained consciousness and wanted another fight. Kurt took the knife offered to him and cut the rope into metre length pieces and then set about tearing the sheets into wide strips.

The thug lying on top of the pile was manhandled roughly and dropped face down onto a nearby sofa. With quick efficiency his wrists were tied behind his back, his ankles tied together before the material strips were used to gag and blindfold him. Now helpless he was unceremoniously dumped in the hallway before the next thug received the same treatment and the next, until all five were lying in the hallway.

We now took our time to straighten Perry's home so that his parents would never guess what had occurred before their return home. Perry left them a note saying that he's gone to stay with me (Danny) for a couple of weeks and would be in contact. The trucks were then brought round the front again and our wriggling captives were carried quickly to the back of the trucks. Then lifted into the back they were secured with more ropes to prevent injury from rolling around and more importantly to prevent escaping. While this was going on Perry and Lewis loaded their bags onto the trucks and climbed up into the cabins. Unfortunately there was little spare room so they had to separate into different trucks, not that they minded too much given the way they eyed up the clan members sitting next to them.

What followed was a more sedate drive back to Gettysburg, taking the expected seven hours with a couple of convenience breaks for the drivers and passengers (but not the captives who remained tied up in the back of the trucks). It was nearly 06:00hrs before we arrived back at the camp totally exhausted and ready to crawl into bed. The only person waiting for us was Ralph who had been kept up to date with regular texts from Kurt. Satisfied that we were all in one piece and unharmed he told us to leave the captives where they were. They would keep until we were ready to deal with them at the next base camp, Green Ridge State Forest. So while we grabbed a few hours sleep the rest of the clan and rally crew packed up ready to drive on when we woke up.

Once we had set up camp in the middle of the State Forest, away from prying eyes, we turned our attention to our captives. They had been bound and gagged for around twelve hours and were now in a filthy state. I held my nose at the stench of their piss and shit soiled clothes. Laughing at my expression Kurt informed me that was all part of the breaking in process, I was to watch and learn!

The captives were dragged roughly from the trucks and dumped unceremoniously onto the ground at the feet of Ralph and Owen who looked at them with disdain.

"So these are the wretches who have been doing the queer bashing?" Owen asked kicking the legs of the nearest captive, who groaned and wriggled in response.

"Yes they are" Kurt confirmed "they've had a good thumping and been left to stew for a while. Question is what do we do with them? The simplest thing would be just to kill them and hide their bodies in the woods, they'd never be found."

This statement drew muffled cries of alarm from the five captives and they renewed their futile struggles to escape making us laugh which added to their alarm.

"Oh no, killing them would be too easy" Owen said as he shook his head deep in thought "I have a better idea. It's been a long time since the clan have had any guard dogs and these mutts might just serve our purposes."

Ralph looked at me and said "Right let's get them some water otherwise they'll die of dehydration before we start."

Nodding I ran over to our trailer, filled up a large bowl with cold water and carried it back to the waiting group having also found a plastic cup. The first captive was pulled to his feet, supported on both sides by Perry and Lewis who had been keen to volunteer in the care (or humiliation) of the captives. Ralph untied the gag, dropped it on the ground before gently placing the water filled cup against the captive's lips. Who being very thirsty eagerly drank from the cup before muttering a 'thank you', as a reward his blindfold was removed before being sat back down on the ground.

He glanced all around himself, taking in the other four captives along with the clan members going about their normal business. Finally he looked in our direction. He immediately recognised Perry and Lewis but took a little longer to recognise Kurt and myself. I for one remembered him as being one of the three queer bashers in the park that evening Kurt and I had encountered. He visibly blanched and avoided our eye contact preferring instead to stare fixedly at his feet.

Turning our attention to the second captive, now stood up, Ralph once again offered him water from the cup. This time although he appeared to swallow the water, he was in fact storing it in his cheeks before with all his might he spat it out in Ralph's face. There was a loud gasp from everyone who saw this, for no one other than perhaps Owen would dare mess with Ralph. Facially he showed no signs of reaction however his hands were a different matter, his right hand formed a fist and he punched the captive hard in the stomach knocking the wind out of him. Then with his left hand he grabbed the man by the throat choking him until he was blue in the face. In what was almost a hiss Ralph told him the next time he spat at anyone, he, Ralph would personally kill him with his bare hands. Releasing his grip on his throat Ralph pushed him onto his knees and removed the blindfold. With Kurt forcibly holding the man's mouth open Ralph casually opened his flies, pulled his flaccid cock out and let a fountain of steaming piss flow into the waiting orifice. Choking on the warm acrid fluid the captive struggled trying to avoid the stream but being held in Kurt's vice-like grip he had no choice but to swallow it. Only when he had finished emptying his bladder did Ralph stop and with a vigorous shake of his cock he slipped it back into his jeans. The captive was placed roughly on the ground next to the first who looked at him in disgust having witnessed the piss drinking.

The other three captives were visibly shaking as one by one they were made to stand up before their gags were removed and offered a cup of water to drink. Having heard Ralph's warning and the wind being knocked out of their comrade along with his subsequent strangled gurgling, they offered no resistance. In fact they acted more like frightened rabbits than the pack of thugs they had been less than twenty four hours ago.

Satisfied that for the moment they were compliant Ralph ordered the removal of their blindfolds and ankle restraints, but their hands remained firmly tied behind their backs. He barked at them telling them to stand up and to follow him as it was time to get them cleaned, the smell of them was disgusting. As they struggled to their feet Ralph strode off downhill in the direction of the nearby stream, which if you listened carefully you could just hear from the camp. Trotting to keep up they looked comical as they tried to avoid bumping into one another and avoiding obstacles along the path. They were closely followed by Perry, Lewis and me for we had been tasked with doing the dirty work with Ralph giving instructions. Kurt and the others stayed behind to construct five individual kennels to house the new dogs.

The stream was perhaps about three feet wide and six inches deep, running swiftly with crystal clear cold water over flattened sandstone pebbles. Having been pre-warned Perry and Lewis stripped to their T-shirts and pants to save their trouser and trainers from getting soaked. Grabbing hold of the nearest captive or 'mutt' as we were now calling them, I dragged him by his shirt collar towards the stream and despite his protests forcibly pushed him into it. Perry was ready for the mutt and with Lewis's help pulled him down until he was laying face up in the stream struggling to keep his face above water. The mutt coughed and spluttered but was ignored as we removed first his shoes and then his socks. Turning our attention to his trousers we unbuttoned it and then unzipped his flies before pulling them roughly down his legs, his shorts too were quickly removed leaving him naked from the waist down. Ralph handed me his pocket knife and before the mutt's frightened eyes I quickly cut his shirt away from his body leaving him stark naked with his hands tied behind his back. The other mutts, being true friends, laughed at his embarrassment as we hauled him to his feet and then soaped him up all over before dunking him in the stream again.

No longer stinking the mutt was released and told to stand over by Ralph and let the warm air dry him off. This procedure was repeated on the other four mutts, despite their half-hearted protests, and in no time at all we had five naked guys shivering as they slowly dried in the breeze.

"When do we get our clothes back? This is kidnap and abuse, we'll get you for this!" Mutt3 grumbled (he had been the one to spit at Ralph earlier on.

Ralph gave a little smile and said "oh really?"

Before Mutt3 could respond Ralph gave him a resounding slap across the face which sent the lad sprawling to the ground.

"Rule number one" Ralph announced as his smile turned into a sneer "you don't say anything unless spoken to. Rule number two, you don't ask questions. If we want you to know something we will tell you. Rule number three, don't ever threaten me or any member of the clan. Next time you do it will be the last mistake you ever make. Understood?"

He cracked his knuckles as if to emphasise his point. All five lads slowly nodded avoiding eye contact with each other and us. I have to admit I was getting a big kick out of being part of the queer bashers' humiliation. Ralph too appeared to be enjoying the situation for having lit a cigarette he stepped over to Mutt4 and blew smoke in his face. Then casually he fondled the lad's balls and played with his cock until he became erect to his obvious embarrassment. Blushing bright red Mutt4 could not help but respond and tried to thrust his hard on into Ralph's hand. Laughing Ralph took his hand away and walked over to a nervous looking Mutt2. Standing behind the lad Ralph bent him over at the waist, then having licked his index finger he felt for the lad's anus and forcefully shoved his finger up inside. The poor lad yelled and went a deeper shade of red, clearly in pain.

"Mmm that's made my day!" Ralph chuckled "A virgin, I shall enjoy having you later."

Mutt2 blanched white at this announcement momentarily forgetting the pain in his backside, until Ralph pulled his finger out. Wincing he stood upright and looked straight into the smirking face of Mutt3.

"Don't worry about it young man, I can be gentle if you do as your told" Ralph said patting Mutt2 on his bum "Now as for you Mutt3, I'm going to wipe that smirk off your face."

Without any warning Ralph grabbed Mutt3's bollocks and gave them a hard squeeze causing the lad to scream in pain. As he opened his mouth Ralph shoved the index finger which had just been up Mutt2's rectum straight into the orifice and wiped it around the inside and over the tongue to clean the shit off. Releasing his grip on Mutt3's balls Ralph wiped his saliva covered finger over the lad's face before giving him a hard shove sending his crashing to the floor for a second time. The look of disgust on the lad's face and his subsequent retching was comical and it took several minutes for us to stop laughing.

As the laughter subsided we heard footsteps approaching, looking in the direction of the sound I saw Kurt and Logan sauntering over to join us. Kurt was carrying what looked like five metal hoops and Logan was carrying five lengths of chain. The five lads looked nervously in the direction of the newcomers and what they were carrying. Lewis grinned having put two and two together and ran over to Kurt to examine the hoops more closely. Perry and I joined him just in time to see Kurt demonstrate how the hoops were actually two hinged semi-circles which interlocked at the open ends and could if desired be secured by a padlock.

Stepping over to the nearest lad (Mutt1) Kurt opened the hoop wide and then carefully closed it around the lad's neck. From his jean's pocket he retrieved a large brass padlock and beckoned Logan over. Taking a length of chain he quickly slipped the padlock's shackle through the last link of the chain and the hoop's interlocking fastener then locked the padlock.

Holding the other end of the chain Kurt silently walked over to Ralph dragging Mutt1 by the neck as he had failed to react quickly enough. Mutt1 glared at the two men in response to this latest humiliation, forgetting what had happened to Mutt3 only moments ago. Ralph grabbed the lad's balls and pulled him roughly towards him, yelping from the pain Mutt1 stumbled trying to stop the pain emanating from his crotch.

"Is there something you want to say?" Ralph growled menacingly.

"No, no, nothing..... Yeow!" Mutt1 cried as Ralph squeezed his balls again.

"No what? Think carefully, wrong answer and I'll rip your little bollocks off" Ralph said smiling this time.

"No.... Sir!"

"Correct answer. Now be a good lad and kneel down by my side like the good little dog you will become."

Mutt1 wisely said nothing. He just glanced at Ralph fearfully before kneeling down as best he could without falling over as his hands were still tied behind his back. Within a few minutes the other four lads were also collared and chained before being brought over to sit at Ralph's feet along with Mutt1.

"Before we lead you to your new home, do any of you need to relieve yourselves?" Ralph asked the five lads.

No one responded.

"You won't get another chance until this evening, so I'll ask that question again. Do you need a piss or a shit?"

This time they nodded, having looked at one another in alarm and embarrassment, before confirming that they did.

Kurt told them to stand up now if they needed to urinate and in response Mutts 1, 2 and 5 stood up making their chains rattle as they did so. Taking hold of their chains Kurt led them to a nearby tree and told them to piss up against the tree trunk. Confused they just looked at him and then one another.

"What are you waiting for?" Kurt growled.

"Uh Sir, our hands are still tied" Mutt5 said with a tremble in his voice.

"So? You don't have to hold your cock to piss. Now get on with it, stop wasting time otherwise I'll think you don't want to go at all" Kurt said pulling on their chains.

Taking his threat seriously the three lads stood in a semi-circle and with expressions of concentration on their faces they sprayed their urine against the trunk. I stood to one side and watched the urine trickle down the bark in golden rivulets but my eyes were drawn to their skinny frames and small bums as their cheeks clenched forcing their bladders to empty quickly. As the fountains slowed to a trickle and then droplets Kurt yanked on the chains, leaving them in no doubt who was boss and forcing them to follow him back up towards the camp.

As they left Ralph confirmed with the remaining two lads that they wanted to defecate. They nodded and stood up assuming that they wouldn't be given long to see to the call of nature. Nodding with a satisfied smile Ralph led them to the edge of the clearing to where a few scrubby bushes grew.

"Remember this spot lads for this is going to be your defecating patch while we are based here" he instructed. "If we catch you soiling anywhere else we'll rub your noses in it, understand?"

"Yes sir" the two lads replied in unison.

"Well get on with it then."

"What right now with them watching?" Mutt4 asked looking in our direction.

"Yep, believe me this is nothing compared to what these guys have had to do before an audience" Ralph said throwing us a knowing grin.

Shrugging his shoulders Mutt3 turned his back to us and squatted down in front of the nearest bush. Ironically this gave us the best view of his backside and the brown log which appeared a couple of seconds later, hung there for a moment before dropping into the grass beneath. Mutt 4 realised that he had no choice but to do the same, squatted next to Mutt3 and emptied his bowels too.

"How am I going to wipe my arse clean?" Mutt3 asked frowning.

"Do what other dogs do, wipe your arse on the ground cover plants but watch out for the stinging nettles!" Logan called out laughing at the thought.

"That's right, or you can wash yourself in the stream. It's up to you." Ralph informed them "Either way hurry up. I've got things to be getting on with and I'm not acting as dog sitter all day!"

Standing up, being careful to avoid their own turds the two lads stepped over to a patch of long grass and did their best to wipe their dirty cracks on the plants. After a few minutes of ungainly shuffling around they stood up and confirmed that they were finished. With a simple nod Ralph led the way pulling the two lads roughly along with their chains to join their comrades. Perry, Lewis and I followed on discussing the surprise turn of events this morning and how we had actually found it arousing watching our previous tormentors being thoroughly humiliated.

Their humiliation hadn't finished yet as we found out when we arrived back at base camp. In our absence the others had built a make shift wooden structure, it looked like a kennel but the size of a small shed. It had a roof and walls on three sides leaving the front open to view. Inside were the five lads, attached by their chains to a central supporting post, with their hands still tied behind their backs and gagged once again.

Looking around us it seemed that everyone had returned to their normal routines. I saw Kurt and Logan walking off with Ralph in the direction of Owen's trailer so we were left to amuse ourselves. A thought occurred to me and with a sly grin I turned to Perry and Lewis inviting them to join in with a little game I had devised. Their grins matched mine in anticipation and together we strode into the kennel. I approached Mutt2 as I found him the most attractive of the lads, dirty blonde hair with blue eyes and the least skinny. As I knelt down in front of him I told him to relax and spread his legs apart, he gave me a wary look but adjusted his position accordingly. This exposed his package to me, his balls hung loosely between his thighs and his decent sized cock hung flaccid over them.

I reached out and gently cupped his balls in one hand and with the other massaged his cock to erection. Mutt2 gave me a look crossed between alarm and arousal but I ignored his gaze and carried on stroking his by now erect cock. While I was doing this Perry and Lewis were doing the same thing to Mutt1 and Mutt5 respectively although initially they had greater difficulty arousing their victims. Eventually though they too had their lads groaning behind their gags begging for release, which we granted once we had grown bored of wanking them off. Now for part two of my scheme! Each of us hand a small handful of jism, Perry and Lewis then with their empty hand undid their trousers and pushed them down around their ankles. Already sporting erections they used the jism to lubricate their cocks, sharing mine between them I walked over to Mutt3. He must have thought he was going to receive the same treatment as he sat there erect with his legs spread, despite his previously homophobic attitude. He was therefore caught by surprise when instead of stroking his cock I pushed him hard backwards and rolled him onto his front. Wasting no time I pinned him down while Perry knelt down and spread Mutt3's legs with his knees. Mutt3 tried to resist by clenching his cheeks, but I slapped them hard shocking him into relaxing them long enough for Perry to aim his cock at the puckered little anus hiding in the hairy crack. Having found the target Perry slowly but forcefully pushed his cock up the virginal tract bringing a lot of muffled cries from Mutt3. Judging by his red face and thrashing around he wasn't enjoying being fucked one little bit.

Perry ignored Mutt3's struggles and gave himself over to fucking the life out of the lad beneath him. Satisfied that Mutt3 was unable to prevent his ordeal I turned my attention to Mutt4 who had retreated in fear as much as the chain would allow him. Not far enough however to prevent his anal virginity being taken by Lewis, this time in the missionary position to give Mutt4 something to think about, so Lewis said.

Someone must have noticed our absence because just as Perry and Lewis were building up to their climax we heard the deep voice of Owen asking.

"What's going on here then?"

Turning to face him I saw the clan elder standing there with hands on hips looking highly amused by the scene of the two mutts being fucked while the other three watched with both fear and interest. Quickly I explained to him that it was my fault as I had thought up this little game.

"Excellent thinking Danny, they will need breaking in anyway. They're going to be used by any clan member or rally crew as desired so they might as well get used to it from the start. Carry on, I like your style!"

Owen chuckled, clapping me on the shoulder before walking off shaking his head as he did so. Free to carry on my two friends resumed their fucking until with triumphant grunts they shot their loads deep into the previously virgin arses. Once they had regained their composure Perry and Lewis pulled their subsiding cocks, still leaking a like jism from the quick to clamp shut anuses of their victims. Lewis had a look of disgust on his face as he glanced down at his cock.

"Uh! The dirty dog has left his shit on my shaft, it stinks!" he said to no one in particular.

"Yeah, mine doesn't smell too fresh either. I thought they both had a dump before coming here" Perry announced as he gingerly inspected his cock.

"They did" I agreed "but they didn't get properly cleaned out though. The dogs have been negligent in their hygiene so I think it's only fair that they volunteer to clean you up properly. What do you think mutts?"

I looked over at Mutt3 and Mutt4 as I said this. Warily and still shaken from their recent ordeal they nodded slowly before glancing at one another. Turning to my friends I suggested that they remove the gags and let the dogs lick them clean. This drew smiles from my friends but grunts of protest from the two lads which needless to say were ignored completely. Lewis undid Mutt4's gag and pushed his now flaccid brown streaked cock towards the closed mouth.

Realising that we might have a battle of wills here I knelt down next to Mutt4 and grabbed his bollocks firmly giving them a slight tug.

"Now open up like a good dog and lick your own dirt of my friend's cock. Lick it nice and clean otherwise I will, and I mean will, rip your bollocks off. What are you waiting for?" I growled at him.

Despite the sickened look on the lad's face he did eventually open his mouth and tentatively stick his tongue out towards the offending item. This was all Lewis needed, for with a satisfied "good boy" thrust his hips forward driving his cock straight into the open mouth, then before Mutt4 could react Lewis grabbed hold of his head to prevent him pulling away. Mutt4 struggled for several minutes gagging not only on the foul tasting slime on the cock but also on the obvious erection as Lewis started to face fuck him.

While this drama had played out Perry had been doing the same with Mutt3, who being a quick learner and already threatened with castration a couple of times simply opened his mouth once the gag had been removed. I was pleased to see that threats of violence would not be needed on this occasion. Sometime later after the two had shot their loads down the less than willing throats we left the five lads in peace to no doubt discuss their ordeals and made our way back to my trailer.

Waiting for us it seemed like half the clan were there in the living area, the elders seated with the younger members standing around appearing a little bored.

"At last the three musketeers return from their adventures!" Logan grinned with a wink at Perry.

"Sorry about that" I started apologetically "we got a little side tracked, helping our new pets get settled in."

"Mmm that's one way of putting it" Kurt replied drily "let's hope none of you catch kennel cough!"

Dexter laughed and added "Do I detect just a hint of jealousy by any chance Kurt?"

"None whatsoever, I've got my own bitch to see to my needs" he laughed giving me a very direct look.

Once again I thanked my genetic inheritance as I blushed crimson as everyone in the room laughed at my expense knowing exactly that Kurt had meant me.

"Okay, okay. Leave the poor guy alone" Owen said softly as he stood up and clapped his hands to gain the attention of the crowded room.

As silence fell he continued "I've asked you all here to let you know about our recent acquisition of five potential clan dogs. This came about after we received a request for help in Glen Falls by these two charming young men" and pointed to Perry and Lewis.

"You may or may not have seen them around this morning being, shall we say "introduced" into their new life with us. For the time being their home is the wooden kennel at the rear of the camp. I'm looking for volunteers to train, walk and possibly home them once they are ready for integration into the clan. Please indicate if you would like to volunteer and in what capacity" Owen concluded sitting back down on the sofa.

The room erupted into an excited hubbub of talk and gesticulating, then as if an unspoken decision had been made the clan members filed out of the trailer and over to the kennel. When we got there I was a little surprised to see the five lads had huddled up as best they could to keep warm. On reflection I shouldn't have been surprised really considering the fact that they were still naked and no one had offered them a blanket or anything to keep them warm. One could say this was part of the master plan to show them who was boss and make them more grateful when some kindness is shown them. They appeared to be asleep so we simply stood looking in from the front so as not to disturb them, how cute they looked. No one would have guessed that only twenty four hours ago they had been threatening to kill my best friends, and before that me! Oh how the tables had turned.

Only the interested parties returned to the trailer to volunteer their services to Owen, who made the following decisions:

(a) The Kennel Master would be Lewis, a fitting revenge on his tormentors.
(b) Dog Walkers would be Kurt, Logan, Dexter, Ralph and Wayne as they would be strong enough to handle any rebellious behaviour should it arise.
(c) Dog Feeders would be me and Perry. It would be our duty to feed the dogs in the morning and evening after they had gone for their walks.

Owen would be in overall charge as he is with the clan members.

By now it was early afternoon and I for one was starving so volunteering like the hero that I am I cooked a fry up for Kurt, Logan, Perry and myself as everyone else had left. Lewis had left with Owen which raised a few eyebrows, I just assumed that they were talking doggy business. Sitting around the dinner table it became very obvious that Logan and Perry were attracted to one another, you didn't need to be an expert in body language to see the mutual lust in their eyes. Sure enough, as Kurt cleared the table the two of them made their excuses and disappeared into Logan's bedroom. Kurt winked at me and tiptoed after them only to return grinning informing me that Logan had put a "Do not disturb" sign on the door handle. As if we couldn't guess what they were doing!

Left to alone Kurt and I spent the next couple of hours on the sofa, wrapped in each other's arms. Relaxed and contented I drifted off to sleep on more than one occasion, only stirring when I felt Kurt move next to me. At one point I felt him squeeze me tight and mutter under his breath "Goddamit, I love you my little cub". Sleepily I sighed and whispered "I love you too daddy bear".

Chuckling he kissed me and then checked his watch, twenty minutes before the dogs were due to be walked. Just enough time for me to give him a blow job, apparently, as he pushed my head towards the bulge in his jeans. As I unzipped his flies and pulled his jeans and jock-strap down his thighs I breathed in his manly aroma and sight of his package. It was something I never tired of looking at or exploring with my mouth even when he wasn't too fresh.

Amid words of encouragement from Kurt I lovingly licked his balls clean of their salty sweat and then focused on the rock hard cock lying along his hairy stomach pointing towards his navel. Lapping at it like it was my favourite lolly I was so wrapped up in this activity I failed to notice that we were no longer alone. Until that is, just as I took his cockhead in my mouth and slipped it down my throat I heard a quiet little giggle to one side. Without interrupting my head bobbing I glanced over to where I had heard the sound. There stood Perry and Logan freshly showered wearing just towels around their waists and clearly enjoying the entertainment I was providing.

Keeping my head in place with one hand Kurt told Logan that he wouldn't be much longer, perhaps he ought to get dressed as the dogs were due to walked very shortly. Logan's grin vanished in an instance obviously he had forgotten for he spun on his heels and disappeared into his bedroom followed closely by Perry. By the time they returned fully dressed I had swallowed Kurt's jism and sucked him dry, a finishing touch he always enjoyed.

After the men had left to walk the dogs Perry and I worked in the kitchen preparing the dog's dinners. Tempting though it was to literally feed them dog food, we were under strict orders to provide them with a meal that we would be happy to eat ourselves. So bearing in mind their hands were still tied behind their backs we prepared a burger meal complete with fries and side salad on large plastic plates. The food was then cut up into bite size portions and left on the dining table ready for their return to camp. While we waited Perry and I sat on the trailer steps enjoying the afternoon sun and compared notes on our men in bed. By the sound of it Logan was as much of an animal as Kurt and from Perry's wistful expressions he enjoyed the sex as much as I did.

The men returned with the five dogs walking before them, clearly still no happier with their situation from their expressions but from their body language much of their resistance had gone. I sauntered over to Kurt deliberately ignoring the dogs and asked how the walk had gone.

"Very well actually" he replied with a smile "they're quick learners. I didn't have to remind them about having a piss and a shit. We'd only gone about 200m out of the camp when they relieved themselves. Washing was a different matter although they stank they were less than keen to bathe in the stream."

"Oh you do surprise me" I replied picturing the scene in my head.

"But you know me, I can be persuasive and soon enough all five had washed. Isn't that right you little mutts?" Kurt laughed as he turned to face the five lads in question.

"Yes Sir" they replied sullenly.

"Cheer up mutts for it's your dinner time!" Perry announced theatrically before climbing into our trailer.

Five faces broke into smiles at the thought of food and seemed keen to return to their kennel judging by the way they pulled at their chain leads. Once they were safely tied to the post again Perry and I fetched their meals and set the plates down in front of them on the floor along with five bowls of fresh water.

"Hey! What about our hands? How are we supposed to eat?" Mutt4 asked struggling to keep his tone polite.

"Well dogs don't have hands. You're bright lads, work it out for yourselves" Ralph replied before ushering us out of the kennel.

Walking away I asked why they still had their hands tied behind their backs and was told that there was still resistance in them, after all they had only been with us for just over a day, so it was risky as they were likely to attempt an escape. This mustn't happen as the police would become involved which they wanted to avoid at all costs. Kidnapping is a serious offence in the eyes of the law. Ralph then casually dropped a bombshell into the conversation, Levi and Sanun would be paying us a visit tomorrow. Beyond that he wouldn't be drawn as to the purpose of their visit. Neither would Kurt when I quizzed him later that evening as we lay cuddled together in bed.

Chapter 12 – The tail that wags the dog

In hindsight I should have known why Levi would be visiting, for what does he specialise in? Tattoos and specialist adult toys of course! Although it had only been a week since we left them in Colonie they greeted us as if we were long lost friends. After exchanging hugs and back slaps Levi retrieved two hold all bags from the back of his truck.

Later that afternoon gathered together in Ralph's trailer we stood round Levi and his bags and peered over his shoulder as he opened the first bag to reveal its contents. First to be removed were what to me looked like pairs of black footballs connected with black laces. Levi passed a couple of balls around the group for closer inspection. When it got to me the first thing that struck me was how soft the ball felt in my hands. The outer casing felt like PVC with the inside squashy as if filled with sponge. Rotating it in my hands I realised that I had overlooked something fundamental in its design which on initial inspection looked like a puckered anus with a leather collar around the ring. Noting my surprised expression Levi invited me to push my hand inside the ball, as I did so Sanun sat down next to me and once my hand was inside the ball he demonstrated to me and the group how the ball could be secured around the wearer's wrist preventing the hand's removal. With my hand trapped inside what was in effect a giant glove I quickly appreciated how disabling it would be if both hands were gloved simultaneously.

"Exactly my friend!" Levi confirmed as he saw the penny drop in my expression "It will be more comfortable for the lads but at the same time will make them feel even more dependent on us."

With grins and nodding heads of understanding from all round Levi returned his attention to the bags at his feet, the first was now empty and put to one side. Carefully he opened the bag so as not to reveal its contents and pulled out several pairs of various sized heavy duty denim shorts, with zipped flies and curiously each had reinforced hole in the seat. All became clear when Levi continued to empty the bag revealing small and medium sized butt plugs with screw threads in the necks. They were followed by incredibly realistic looking dog tails in a variety of shapes and colours.

Lewis clapped enthusiastically and laughed in delight as he examined the tails selecting the ones he considered good matches for the five recipients. As Levi demonstrated how the three items fitted together Lewis looked over at Ralph and said

"We will of course have to see which size plug will fit best with each dog. I'm going to enjoy doing that no end!"

"Perhaps we should film the tail fittings for posterity? They could then be added to the film footage we already have" Sanun said in a detached professional tone.

"Excellent" Ralph replied "I'm looking forward to seeing the finished video!"

"Then of course there is the small matter of the dog's tattoos. We could film that too" Levi added as he packed away the shorts and tails which weren't required.

It was decided that the fittings would happen after the dogs had had their evening walk but before they'd eaten, that way they'd be empty for receiving the plugs and too hungry to object to the wearing the hand mittens. In preparation the clan members who weren't dog walking organised a barbecue and seating so that everyone would get a good view of the proceedings. Perry and I prepared the dog's dinners, small bite size sandwiches along with chopped salad again laid out on plastic plates to prevent breakages.

As the sun slipped behind the tree tops Kurt and the others returned with their dogs leading the way, keen to get back because they knew they would be fed next. The other four dog walkers hung back as Kurt led Mutt3 over to Levi who untied the lad's wrists. Pleased to have his hands free Mutt3 massaged his wrists and pin-wheeled his arms to loosen up his arm's muscles, however he wasn't so happy when Lewis and Perry presented the hand mittens to him.

"What are those for?" he asked warily.

"You'll find out soon enough" Lewis replied as he took hold of Mutt3's wrist and pushed the mitten over the lad's hand.

Then with quick almost practised movements Perry secured the wrist fastenings before Mutt3 could pull away. I watched the lad's expression and I was surprised to see no trace of defiance, just resignation as if he knew freedom was a long way off. Just as quickly his other hand was enclosed in the mitten, now he looked like a naked boxer but without the fighting spirit. Wanting to be part of the action I picked up one of the denim shorts which I judged to be of the right size and waved them in front of the lad telling him he could now put them on. Happy at the thought of wearing clothes again he was keen to co-operate, lifting his feet into the legs of the shorts he said a 'thank you' as I pulled them up. Little did he know what was to follow!

Kurt joined us and with one hand grabbed Mutt3's metal collar and pushed it downwards. This forced the lad first to bend over at waist then as Kurt knelt on the ground he sank to his knees with his head resting on the ground and bum high in the air. Lewis had in the meantime collected a medium sized butt plug and black tail to match Mutt3's close cropped black hair. With Levi holding a small can of Crisco Lewis scooped out a wad of the white grease and smeared it all over the butt plug before smearing more all around the lad's anus after Perry had pulled the shorts down around Mutt3's knees. He clenched his cheeks in protest of this treatment but resistance was futile because as soon as he tired of clenching Lewis pushed the butt plug into the crack and placed the plug's tip against the anal ring.

Before he could react Lewis pushed hard on the plug, with a cry of pain from Mutt3 the butt plug disappeared up inside his rectum and his anus clamped down hard on the plug's neck. Perry pulled the shorts back up, fed the shaft of the tail through the hole in the short's seat before screwing it onto the butt plug. Kurt pulled the stunned lad upright and once standing fastened the shorts waistband and did the zip up taking care not to catch his tackle in the process.

It was now the turn of the other four to have their mittens and tails fitted. Seeing how calm Mutt3 had behaved this seemed to set a precedent and one by one they surrendered to being transformed into human dogs bearing the indignity with stoic silence. Once all five were done they were led back to their kennel where their food was waiting for them. Having chained them up for the night the dog walkers rejoined the group and the barbecue began in earnest with large quantities of food and beer being consumed.

With the food eaten talk turned to the subject of tattoo designs and when the lads would be tattooed. Due to time constraints Levi would have to do all five tomorrow, making it essential that the tattoos be relatively simple. After much discussion Owen decided the tattoo wording should be 'Guard Dog' emblazoned across their shoulder blades with 'Honaw Bitch' on their biceps in the same style as the clan members. Both messages would be equally true.

The following morning the dogs were fed and walked as normal, from the dog walkers' feedback keeping the butt plugs in overnight had been very effective. Having emptied both their bladders and bowels all five were fucked by the dog walkers, again to reinforce who was in charge. With their anal rings stretched around the plugs for nearly twelve hours, the lads were able to accommodate the impaling cocks easily and even seemed to enjoy the action judging by how easily they spontaneously shot their loads while being fucked. Before returning to the camp the plugs were reinserted and shorts pulled up again.

Instead of being taken back to their kennel they were led over to Ralph's trailer where Levi and Sanun were waiting for them with the tattooing machinery and five syringes of the anally administered anaesthetic. One by one on Levi's command the lads bent over in front of him, had their tails and shorts removed before having the anaesthetic squirted up their backsides. As they passed out from the anaesthetic we carried them through to the bedroom where they were kept while waiting to be tattooed. I left them to it for having experienced the process myself I wasn't in a hurry to witness it.

Later that evening the five lads emerged from Ralph's trailer looking disorientated and in pain. Once again their dog tails had been reinserted and the denim shorts were being worn. Word quickly spread through the camp and before they were half way back to their kennel they had been surrounded by the clan members all intent on examining the lads tattoos. Levi stood proudly watching from the sidelines as we praised him on his handiwork for the tattoos were, as ever, very exquisitely inked and coloured. As the lads stood in a row I really couldn't tell any difference between them for the designs had been drawn on so professionally and consistently.

Owen joined the lads in their kennel and as they ate their evening meal off their plates on the floor, using only their mouths, he told them that he was pleased with their progress so far. He went on to explain that if they promised to behave themselves that this would be their last night sleeping in the kennel and having to wear their mittens and dog tails. This latest piece of information really cheered them up, enough for them to stop eating and clap their mittens together before grinning with dirty chins. Leaving them in peace to finish their food he smiled as he passed us gathered at the kennel entrance curious to know what he had in mind.

The following morning we found out, for he had planned with Lewis the next stage of their training. After their customary walk in the morning they returned to camp naked once more but carrying their mittens, dog tail and shorts. Standing in a row before Owen and the clan, they were finally freed from the metal chains they had been attached to since being brought to this camp. The collars would remain in place until their training had finished, to serve as a reminder of their position in the camp, as if their tattoos would let them forget!

Owen announced that during the day they were going to be taught about how the clan organises the motorcycle rallies, their role within it and what would be expected from them. They would also receive martial arts training for their primary purpose would be to ensure the public behaved during the rallies and to stamp out any trouble should it arise, without using weapons. During the evening they will 'lodge' with the dog walkers sleeping wherever they are permitted. They will also be allowed to wear regular clothes again. All this would be available to them on three conditions which were (1) not to attempt to escape, (2) to remain loyal to the clan and (3) to obey any requests made or instructions or given to them.

With such an offer laid before them not one of the lads refused the offer and accepted the conditions happily. Clearly getting out of the kennel and being treated like a human again was very important to them. I looked over to Kurt and saw him smiling broadly happy with the idea of having one of the lads lodging with us. The trailer was going to be crowded tonight for there would be Kurt and I in one bedroom, Logan and Perry in another and two lads in the living area. No privacy for me then I thought to myself. I was right but not quite in the way that I had imagined.

With agreement reached the five lads were given clothing donated by various clan members who were near enough the same size. From their expressions they obviously found it strange to be wearing clothes again and it seemed to be a turning point for them. Their attitude towards the clan members changed from being resentful of their treatment to being one of the gang. With a slight cockiness in their stride they joined the clan elders in Owen's trailer to start their training and absorption into the clan. I made a comment regarding this to Lewis and Perry hoping that this wasn't going to prove to be a step too far too quickly. Lewis shook his head and assured me that their resistance had been broken and were almost converted to a gay lifestyle. I laughed at this suggestion but Lewis was serious he had come to the conclusion that they all had gay tendencies which had been buried beneath layers of homophobic indoctrination. I just had to hope he was correct as I would be sleeping in a trailer with two of them, I didn't fancy being battered to death during the night.

Shortly afterwards Levi and Sanun returned to Colonie having bid us an emotional farewell for we weren't due to return to their neck of the woods until this time next year when the annual rally circuit was repeated. With everyone seemingly occupied with either the new guard dogs or their own business I felt at a loose end, so I spent the rest of the afternoon writing catch up emails to my parents and then because I was totally bored I actually cleaned and tidied the trailer up from one end to another.

It was evening before Kurt, Logan and Perry returned with two of the lads, Mutt1 and Mutt2, filling the silent trailer with laughter and dirty jokes as they flopped out onto the sofas. Only Kurt greeted me directly by coming over to where I stood in the kitchen, gave me a big bear hug and lingering kiss on the lips before whispering in my ear that he loved me and had missed me this afternoon. Looking into his handsome face I whispered back that I loved him too.

Feeling like a domestic goddess I first gave everyone including myself a bottle of cold beer from the fridge before joining them. Sitting on the floor between Kurt's outstretched thighs I casually asked the others how the afternoon had gone. What followed was an hour long re-enactment of the training session and the debate over the five lads' new names which all had to be dog related. Mutt1 was now called 'Doban', Mutt2 'Reiller', Mutt3 'Alsat', Mutt4 'Bumas' and Mutt5 'Rasil'. I grinned at the names for it didn't take a genius to guess the origins of the names but my grin faded as Doban and Reiller frowned before informing me that they themselves had chosen the names as a way of breaking the link to their former selves. I apologised and changed the subject swiftly perhaps Lewis had been correct about their re-orientation after all.

A little later I cooked the evening meal of curry, rice and poppadoms (okay most of it was out of a jar, but it still looked and tasted good) and played being the host. I could see Kurt giving me curious looks from time to time, perhaps wondering what my game was, but in all honesty after being alone all afternoon it was nice to have the company and do something for them. My reward for such hard labour was to relax and snuggle up next to Kurt on the sofa and watch a soccer match while the others washed and wiped up before playing poker round the dining table.

Chapter 14 – Three in a bed

At the end of the soccer game Kurt casually mentioned that for the next few nights Reiller would be sleeping in our bed with us as part of his training. I was a little surprised I have to admit by this development and his casual announcement, but this is Kurt we're talking about so I should have known better.

Raising an eyebrow I asked drily "This training, would it by any chance be similar to that I received from you?"

Smirking just a little he replied "Uh huh."

"And would you perhaps need assistance with this training?"

"Uh huh, but only if you want to, no pressure like" Kurt's smirk grew into a smile.

"Well it's only fair. It's been a long day and I wouldn't want you to bear the burden all on your own...." I trailed off with a grin matching his.

"That's what I love about you. Not only are you good looking and horny as hell but you're always thinking about my wellbeing" he chuckled as he kissed me on the forehead.

"That's me, I just can't help it!" I replied as I snaked a hand inside his waistband heading for his packet.

"Come on let's go have a shower and get in the mood for a little tuition" Kurt said before rising and pulling me up with him.

Having bid everyone goodnight I headed for the bathroom while Kurt wandered over to Reiller to inform him of the sleeping arrangements. Out of the corner of my eye I saw Reiller's startled expression before he shrugged his shoulders and nodded his understanding. Kurt was hot on my heels and I had only just got into the shower when he joined me under the jet of water, ensuring that we had an intimate and erotic shower together. We had been in bed for nearly twenty minutes before there was a quiet knock on the door and Reiller hesitantly walked into the room.

"Where do I sleep?" he asked looking around the darkened room.

"In bed with us of course" Kurt replied without opening his eyes "and lose the clothes while you're at it."

How did he know Reiller was wearing anything? It was logical I suppose, thinking about it, who would normally walk around naked in a stranger's home especially their bedroom? Unable to resist my curiosity I lifted my head to see Reiller pulling his T-shirt over his head and casually throw it onto the floor by the wardrobes. He then quickly pushed his briefs down, stepped out of them, leaving them where they lay and went to climb into bed.

"Not so fast young man" Kurt said sternly "you're not at home now. There's no mummy to clear up after you. So fold up your clothes and put them neatly into the bottom of the wardrobe, then you can join us."

Sighing Reiller did as he was told before he climbed into the bed lying beside Kurt but as close to the edge as possible.

"Don't be shy, come closer, in fact you can lay in the middle" Kurt said in a reassuring tone.

I felt the bed shift under the weight of the two men as they swapped positions, Kurt had been right about it being cosy for there was little room to move now without touching each other. No doubt this was exactly what he had in mind. We lay there in silence for a few minutes while Reiller did his best to pretend that he had gone straight to sleep. But his body was too tense to fool either of us so wasting no more time Kurt and I began the training session.

Following Kurt's lead I turned to face Reiller and gently ran my hands all over the front of his body while Kurt did the same from behind. Reiller's body initially tensed even further for no doubt he was wary about what was to follow but slowly little by little he relaxed as he realised we weren't going to hurt him. He can't have disliked the contact that much because as my hands explored his thighs, balls and cock he was already rock hard. Taking the initiative I threw the duvet off and slid down the bed until my mouth was millimetres from his cock head. Teasing him for a minute I breathed on him, arousing him further and prompting him to actively take part by taking hold of my head and pushing his cock into my willing mouth.

For the next few minutes Kurt carried on stroking Reiller, allowing me to get into the blow job before he made his move. Reaching into his bedside drawer he retrieved the tube of KY and lubed up his own erection before lubing up Reiller's anus ready for penetration. There was a momentary interruption to my cock sucking while Kurt manoeuvred the lad into position and then carefully crammed his large cock into the small hole. I heard the lad groan from the exertion of trying to accommodate the impalement but noted that not once did he try to pull away. Interesting I thought to myself as I resumed sucking on his cock. Before long Kurt was fully buried inside Reiller and while he waited for the lad to become accustomed to his size I reached over with my spare hand and held Kurt's uppermost cheek in my hand. Now while I sucked on Reiller's cock I could feel Kurt's muscles working as he thrust in and out of his arse. This I had to admit was a becoming a head trip for me then I had an idea.

Pulling off Reiller's cock before he could cum, I retrieved the tube of KY and lubed up my own hole. Reiller's expression changed from frustration as I stopped blowing him to one of happy anticipation as he realised that he was about to fuck me instead. Wasting little time I spooned myself into him and pushed my bum into his crotch. For a minute or two I allowed myself the pleasure of teasing him before unable to control my lust any longer I reached behind me and guided his cock to my anus. With barely a pause for breath I pushed myself backwards until my bum was pressing against his groin and I could get no more of him in me. Reiller was now caught between the two of us and by the sounds that he was making I gathered he was enjoying the ride, both front and back. We carried on like this for a little while until with a stuttered "Aaargh!" Reiller shot his first load of jism up my rectum. His body's shudders tipped Kurt over the edge and with a cry he too shot his load deep into Reiller. We laid there for a few minutes regaining our breath barely saying a word other than to check we were all okay.

Having established that we were, Kurt pulled out of Reiller who went to pull out of me until he was stopped by Kurt's hand and shake of his head.

"No" Kurt said "stay inside Danny. I want you to slowly roll over onto your back with your legs spread wide. Danny I want you to keep Reiller inside you at all times and roll with him until you are upright, then turn around to face him so that you are astride him. Got that?"

We both confirmed that we understood and followed his instructions to the letter. As I sat impaled on his rapidly hardening cock I looked down at Reiller and asked him if he was enjoying himself. He appeared surprised by my concern but with little hesitation he nodded before being distracted by what Kurt was doing behind me. Personally I had already guessed what Kurt would do, having been in this position before with him and Logan. Sure enough I felt Kurt's cock press against my anal ring and then as I relaxed my ring he slid easily up inside me joining Reiller already there. I love the sensation of being double fucked. The feeling of two cocks jostling for position inside me is heavenly especially when the pace picks up and I get fucked hard.

With Kurt pounding my hole hard and fast it didn't take long for my hole to stretch wide open nor for him to shoot his second load of the evening. Unfortunately for Reiller he was in a pretty passive position being unable to actively thrust into me so he had not been able to cum by the time Kurt pulled out still dripping his juice. I was gob-smacked when he mentioned this fact out loud however Kurt took it in his stride and told him that his problem would soon be solved. He climbed off the bed and as I watched I saw him retrieve a familiar looking can of Crisco from the wardrobe and remove the lid as he rejoined us. From his vantage point Reiller couldn't see what Kurt was doing, but I guessed that he was busy greasing up his hand and wrist. Yep, spot on. Having knelt down behind me again I felt fingers feeling their way around my ring and pushing up inside me. Taking deep breaths I waited for the inevitable as more of his fingers slid inside me and wrapped themselves around Reiller's cock. I looked down at him and nearly burst out loud laughing at the look of rapture on his face. Fortunately I managed to choke back the laughter and merely smiled encouragement at him.

At times like this I was glad of the anal training I had received before the initiation ceremony and while staying with Levi and Sanun for it made swallowing Kurt's fist so much easier. With barely a glimmer of discomfort his fist was inside me and busy wanking Reiller off, whose expression changed from rapture to amazement as he realised what was happening.

After he had shot his second load of jism he propped himself up on his elbows, with me still riding him, and asked Kurt if he really had been in me while being wanked off.

"Oh yes indeed" Kurt chuckled looking over my shoulder as his greasy jism coated hand withdrew from my gaping hole.

Reiller's eyes opened wide in shock as he took in the sight of Kurt's dirty hand now held out towards him as evidence.

"Oh my God! I can't believe that's possible!" was all he could say.

"Ah now Reiller, you see us Honaws are talented guys, especially my cub Danny. Would you like to fist him?"

"Is that allowed?" Reiller asked suddenly looking unsure of himself.

"You bet" Kurt casually replied "he likes nothing better than having a guy's fist up his arse."

"Won't I hurt you?" he asked me slowly coming round to the idea.

I looked at his hands and saw that they were quite small so I said "No. I can take Kurt's fists okay so I will be able to take yours."

"Yes please in that case" he said with a dirty smile "my cock loves being in you, I wanna see if my fist does too!"

As there was nothing else to say on the subject I climbed off Reiller and his softened cock slipped out of my sloppy hole without a sound. I crawled on all fours backwards until my knees were almost on the edge of the bed and waited for the two guys as they climbed off and walked round until they were standing behind me. Looking over my shoulder I watched Kurt demonstrate how to thoroughly grease up his hand with Crisco before greasing up my anus.

Reiller watched intently how Kurt coned his fingers and thumb before pushing them up inside me with barely any resistance. Copying Kurt's example to the letter Reiller was soon greased up and guiding his fist into my very sloppy hole. As predicted because his hands were relatively small he had no trouble slipping his fist into me.

"Oh my God!" he exclaimed for the second time this evening "I've got my whole fist in you! Are you sure it doesn't hurt?"

I smiled over my shoulder at him and replied "Not at all, it feels wonderful. Believe me I'll let you know if you're hurting me."

Kurt then stepped closer to Reiller and offered him words of advice on what to do while inside me. In response to Kurt's coaching I felt Reiller's fist open up and his fingers explore the inside of my rectum. I groaned in pleasure as he massaged my prostate making my cock harden in response. It wasn't long before I felt his hand slowly slide further in and his finger tips then found my inner ring. Reiller asked Kurt if he should now pull out assuming that this was as far as he could go. Laughing Kurt told him that the fun had only just begun and like the outer anal ring, the inner ring could be easily breached due to my extensive anal training. Trusting this information Reiller coned his fingers and gently pushed against my inner ring.

Taking deep breaths I focused on relaxing that ring as best I could, then with only slight discomfort I felt his fist slide past the ring and up into my bowels. By now half his forearm was buried within me, again on Kurt's instructions Reiller applied more grease to his arm up to and beyond his elbow. Then slowly and very carefully he pushed further and further into me until I felt his elbow press against my anus and then breached it. Kurt told him to remain stationery to allow me to grow accustomed to the intrusion and for him to get the camera for posterity. After a few clicks of the camera from various angles he told Reiller to continue pushing up inside me. It didn't take long for his elbow to reach my inner ring, thankfully his arm was relatively slender and his elbow was able to pass through my inner ring as easily as his fist had. By now I was beginning to feel full and experience peculiar sensations as his fist slid further up into my torso. Eventually I could take no more and in a hoarse voice asked Reiller to stop pushing.

"Wow man!" he exclaimed in an awed tone "You are not going to believe the pictures when you see them....."

"So how does it feel?" Kurt asked him matter of factly as he continued to take photos of us.

"Like I'm wearing a warm silky glove, all the way up to my shoulder, it's a real head trip for me."

"Yeah that sounds about right" Kurt said nodding his head "but now you've had some fun we need to take care of Danny here who's been very accommodating for us."

Without further ado Kurt scooted underneath me and took my cock into his mouth, sucking it as Reiller slowly pulled out of me. As his elbow slid past my inner ring and hit my prostate I exploded, my pent up jism flooded Kurt's mouth making him choke until his quick swallowing caught up with my output. Reiller's fist left my arse with a very loud squelchy plop followed by some embarrassing wet farts!

No one said a word as we headed towards the bathroom and toilet, the recent session had been mind blowing and we were lost in thought as we washed ourselves clean. As I returned to our bedroom I heard a slapping noise followed by masculine giggles coming from Logan's bedroom, I wondered what on earth was going on behind the door. But bearing in mind our own recent session perhaps it was best not to know. Before we settled down to sleep Kurt connected his camera to his laptop and we watched as a succession of photos charted Reiller's progress. Slowly image by image his arm disappeared inside me until in the last photo his arm pit was only a couple of inches away from my incredibly stretched anus. Now it was my turn to utter an 'oh my God' as the other two studied the photo closely. No wonder I had felt so full and my innards felt sore from all that stretching! Reiller's attitude towards both me and Kurt changed from that moment onwards, he was now more like a kid brother who hung on our every word and did as he was told. I guess you could say he was now the perfect 'dog'.

The next few days followed a similar routine for us, each morning Reiller went off for his martial arts training while Kurt and I enjoyed spending quality time together in peace. Then the evenings were spent socially with the clan before retiring to bed where Reiller's sexual training continued with him being able to accommodate ever larger items up his backside. One day soon he will receive his first fist.

Chapter 15 – On tour

Two incredibly busy months have passed since our vacation in the Green Ridge State Forest. On the business front we held a motorcycle rally at Morgantown, West Virginia before moving on to Kalamazoo, Michigan and then on to Chillicothe, Ohio before finally Lake Ozark, Missouri which is where we are at present.

The five guard 'dogs' have been fully trained and accepted into the clan. They live in their own trailer under the supervision of Lewis, the Kennel Master. By all accounts Lewis is as happy as can be, who wouldn't be? He controls five fit and horny young men now fully versatile in the arts of gay sex and able to give or take as the situation demands. Knowing Lewis as I do, he wants his sex on a daily basis so he will be putting them to good use. Like me, the more he gets the more he wants! They have proved invaluable in their role at eliminating trouble makers. We always get the odd one or two guys who want to throw their weight around but after a normally short 'knock around' with our dogs they soon see the error of their ways and either leave the rally or behave themselves.

Logan and Perry have formalised their relationship with Perry becoming Logan's cub and busy with his anal training ready for the next initiation ceremony. Kurt and Logan have been doing the same to Perry that they did to me, I was invited to join in but the idea of fisting my best friend felt too weird to contemplate. Not that I have been shy about being around when the training has happened. On more than one occasion I have sat on the sofa with my laptop checking emails and surfing the internet while Perry's anus was stretched by cocks, dildos and fists. After his initial embarrassment with me being present he quickly grew accustomed to the situation and finally admitted that he understood why I had run off with Kurt all those months ago.

For me personally this has been the happiest period of my life so far. Kurt and I have grown ever closer as I have learnt more about my bear of a man and if it's possible even more in love with him. Physically I have toughened up as my exercise regime has continued uninterrupted, I will never be as big as Kurt but I definitely have visible muscles now! Not only that I have also learnt to ride a motorbike under Kurt and Dexter's expert tuition. One of the trade stands kindly 'donated' a brand new bike to the clan after the sales manager spent an athletic night with Alsat and Reiller in their trailer. The following morning both lads looked exhausted and neither could walk straight, much to our amusement and the other three dog's envy (Alsat and Reilly each received generous financial bonuses from the clan for their overtime).

Within a couple of weeks I had become sufficiently experienced to join Kurt and the clan elders on their regular excursions out of town. Sometimes it was for a scenic tour of the area and sometimes it was purely urban rides, either way we always met up with other bikers they knew and after a social drink and chat we would return back to our camp. It seemed odd to me that we never took the most direct route back but it wasn't for me to question the elders.

This activity brought me to the brink of losing Kurt's trust and at the same time putting my life at risk. No, I'm not exaggerating but I do suspect that I'm not the brightest bulb in the box. It took me a long time to realise that our cut of the entrance and site fees could not generate the amount of cash I saw floating around the clan. So where did all the extra money come from? Did it have anything to do with our frequent excursions? The more I thought about it the more I became disturbed by this idea and it gnawed away at me until I blurted these very questions out to Kurt as we lay in bed one evening.

I have never seen him react so angrily and aggressively. For a split second I thought he was going to attack me but somehow he retained self-control and simply sat up in bed glaring down at me as he denied everything. Not satisfied with his response I pushed my luck by listing all the things I had witnessed over the last few weeks which simply didn't make sense. I noticed the more I carried on the more his resistance weakened as he realised that I was close discovering the answer for myself.

Holding up his hands in surrender he admitted that the clan did have more than one source of income. The front they presented to the world was the motorcycle rallies and retail sales but in reality this was a fraction of their true income. The main income sources were acting as drug runners and distributors of illegally gained cash. The clan's reputation of discretion, reliability and honesty ensured that they were the vehicle of choice for many gangs across the United States. The flip side to this situation was that once involved there was no going back because the clan could not afford secrets to be leaked, clan members simply knew too much. There was another reason why clan members could never leave, without the clan's protection they face being taken out by rival gangs or by the Police.

I laid there dumbstruck, shocked by his candid admission even though I had already suspected the truth. Then I smiled and pulled Kurt down towards me kissing him passionately once he was close enough. What followed was a frenetic fuck, finally satiated Kurt rolled off me and propped himself up with an elbow.

"So what brought that on?" I asked revelling in the post-fuck sensations washing through my body.

"I guess I realised just how much I love and want you in my life" he replied with a slight smile "I was worried that you would try to leave me and I wanted at least one last fuck before you do."

"I love you too and I'm not about to leave. Where else will I find such a gorgeous guy with huge cock like your?" I replied giving his balls a loving squeeze.

And that folks is how I became involved in laundered money and drugs.

Chapter 16 – The long arm of the law

The next rally was at Depew, Oklahoma and it was there that I discovered the real reason that the clan insisted on its members being able to insert huge objects up their backsides. The second evening we were there Ralph invited me to join him and Kurt in his trailer. Kurt looked on edge and insisted that we were both fully cleaned out before going over to Ralph's. Puzzled I did as I was told without comment, I didn't want another confrontation with him not when he looked so agitated.

Standing next to Kurt in Ralph's living room I felt like a naughty school boy standing in front of the headmaster. Ralph was all business like with no trace of his usual friendliness. Perhaps he didn't like the situation any more than we did or maybe it was simply he knew the risks we faced each time we did a delivery or collection run. Doban had followed us into the trailer and on Ralph's command locked the trailer's front door so that we wouldn't be disturbed.

Doban had become Ralph's favourite and frequently shared his bed at night when his services weren't required elsewhere. Ralph told us to drop our trousers and shorts and then to bend over. Having done so, Doban lightly greased up our anuses with Crisco before carefully pushing several hot-dog sized plastic containers up into our rectums. Each one was securely sealed to prevent spoilage of the contents, in this case rolls of $100 bills. Once Doban had wiped every trace of the Crisco off our backsides we put on our bike leathers and prepared for our journey to Okemah and back. Riding off into the dark night we would be hard to identify, should anybody be watching, for we were dressed in black leathers wearing black helmets and riding black motorcycles. We arrived back at camp some three hours later having taken the back roads to Okemah, expelled the plastic containers at a specified drop off point and had the obligatory drinks with our clients.

I knew that what we were doing was illegal and morally wrong but I got one hell of an adrenalin rush each time we did the runs. I know Kurt felt the same way for whenever we got back to the trailer after a successful run he would virtually drag me into the bedroom and spend the next hour or so fucking and fisting my brains out. And I loved it! To be wanted and so dynamically possessed by the man I adored blew my mind each and every time it happened. Once we were both satiated I would lay wrapped in his muscular arms as we discussed our recent run before drifting off to sleep.

The rally stayed at Depew for a further week before moving on to Alvarado, Texas during which time we did another three runs without incident. However as we crossed the border into Texas the atmosphere within the clan changed becoming more watchful and wary of any strangers loitering around the camp. The guard dogs were placed on high alert and earned their keep seeing off several intruders.

Over breakfast I quizzed Kurt and Logan about this change and what was it about Texas that had caused it. The answer was simply that in the past they had been raided several times by the police. Thankfully each time it had happened the police had found nothing even after turning the trailers upside in their searches. Now they take no chances and do few runs while in the state unless it is for an important client. Unfortunately half way through the rally at Alvarado Owen received a call from the Amadahy Gang, our largest client, who wanted us to contact a local gang to set up a business relationship with them.

Arrangements were made for Kurt and I to scout out the area prior to the meeting with the gang. Our guardian angels must have been watching over us that day, for having only got five miles into our journey to Waxahachie I heard the wailing of a police car's siren. Looking over my shoulder it's red and blue lights were flashing and the front passenger was signalling for us to pull over.

Kurt and I slowed the bikes to a halt and climbed off before removing our helmets, as we did so Kurt winked to signal that we would be fine. That was easy for him to say as my heart thumped loudly in my chest but as we weren't carrying anything illegal what could they do?

The officer's sauntered over to us removing their guns from their belts and aimed them at us.

"Where are you two going?" the officer in charge asked addressing Kurt.

"Just going for a ride in the country, officer" Kurt replied in a neutral tone.

"Don't get lippy with me Honaw boy, we've been watching you" the officer said.

"Well if that's the case then you already know the answer, don't you?" Kurt replied in mock innocence.

The younger officer, perhaps the same age as me, lost his patience with us and said

"Sir, let's cut this bullshit out, we know and they know they're carrying drugs. Why don't we just arrest them and take them back to the station?"

I glanced over in alarm at Kurt at the young officer's suggestion but Kurt didn't seem at all bothered. In fact he taunted the officer by shrugging his shoulders and said

"You're wasting your time but if you've got nothing better to do......"

The young officer growled and took a step towards Kurt but stopped when the senior officer shook his head and held his hand up.

"Mmm I think it's time we called your bluff" he said to Kurt before looking at both of us and continuing "walk over to the squad car, facing it place your hands on the car and spread your legs. Understand? Good, now move slowly and don't do anything stupid."

We did as instructed and as I stood there spread eagled I watched the two lanes of traffic race by, staring back at the vehicles passengers staring at us out of curiosity. The senior officer then thoroughly searched Kurt before searching me too, while this was going on the young officer searched our bikes just as thoroughly. There was something erotic about having a total stranger feeling me all over through my clothes next to a busy highway. I found myself springing an erection just in time for the police officer to reach my crutch, he can't have missed my erection but he made no comment.

"What did you find?" the senior officer asked his colleague.

"Nothing Sir, what about you?" the young officer replied.

"Nothing, either they've hidden the drugs very cleverly in their clothing or they've hidden it in their bodies."

"I said you're wasting your time" Kurt repeated with a distinctly smug smile.

"Time to find out which it is" the senior officer announced.

Over the next half an hour Kurt and I were forced to remove each item of clothing we were wearing until we stood in just our boxer shorts. Methodically and very slowly the two officers examined every inch of our clothes including our socks and boots! Then mirroring Kurt's smug smile the young officer told us to remove our shorts and hand them over. Ever the exhibitionist Kurt made a show of pushing down his shorts and faced the road, egged on by the tooting of car horns and the occasional wolf whistle. Me being shyer I simply slipped them down and faced away from our audience. After a quick inspection of our shorts, the officers concluded that there was nothing hidden in them either.

"Right, I guess it's now down to the body cavity search" the young officer said with a disgusted expression.

He then told us to turn round and face him so that he could look in our mouths and ears. While he did this the senior officer retrieved two pairs of latex gloves and a tube of KY. Satisfied that our mouths and ears were clear they slipped on their gloves and told us to bend over the car bonnet and spread our cheeks with our hands. With the sound of the passing traffic roaring in my ears I felt the cold lubricant being applied to my anus before first one finger and then two slip easily into my rectum and feel all around inside. While the younger officer finished his examination of Kurt as quickly as possible announcing that he'd found nothing the fingers in my arse remained where they were.

The fingers continued stroking my prostate and then I felt the senior officer breathing in my ear before whispering "you love this don't you queer boy?"

"Yes sir" I replied ignoring the insult.

"I bet you love to suck cock too" he said in a louder voice.

"Yes sir" I replied quite truthfully.

"It's your lucky day then" he said as he stood up and wiped his greasy fingers on my bum.

"Why?" I asked warily.

"I get my cock sucked and you get to go on your way with just a warning" he said laughing at his own humour and undoing his flies.

The young officer looked at his colleague in surprise but not wanting to miss out on the opportunity to dump his load he gestured to Kurt to get down on his knees in front of him. So five minutes later there was Kurt and me, naked by the side of a busy highway, on our knees giving the two officers a blow job! Using our best techniques we quickly brought the two men to orgasm and swallowed their jism without spilling a drop of the sweet yet salty fluid.

The senior officer was true to his word, as he stuffed his now flaccid cock back into his trousers he warned us to be careful for the next police officer we came across might not be so amenable. The police were watching our every move in Texas and just looking for an excuse to throw us in jail.

Given our clothes back we dressed making small talk with them but I had to laugh to myself for the young officer simply could not meet our eyes. Perhaps he regretted talking part in some queer boy action!

We sat on our bikes with the engines running and waited for the police officers to drive off, once out of sight Kurt called Owen on his mobile and told him about our encounter with the law. The response from Owen was to call the job off for one day and inform the Amadahy Gang that another way would have to be found to complete the business deal. Having terminated the call Kurt turned towards me and burst out laughing, I grinned in response and we high fived before rejoining the highway and heading for home. This was my first brush with the law and I'm sure it won't be my last. With luck on my side Kurt and I will have a long and exciting life together. Just what I wished for all those months ago.

www.ingramcontent.com/pod-product-compliance
Lightning Source LLC
Chambersburg PA
CBHW080718120726
48001CB00010B/3070